MW01199264

Printed by Create Space, an Amazon.com Company

www.dejavoodoobook.com

This book is lovingly dedicated to my husband Kenneth. You inspired me to make this vision become a reality. Thank you for the infinite ways you lift me up.

Déjà VooDoo
By
Leslie Brown

Chapter 1

Being cursed sucks! I'm not talking about the guy I beat to the front row parking spot at the Piggly Wiggly calling me a bitch last week. I'm talking about a real Voodoo curse that I inherited at birth along with my twin sister. I drove through town, top down on my Jeep just running a few errands. It started out to be a perfectly normal day, yeah, normal. Pick up the U-Haul trailer, a quick trip to a witch's shop and a Voodoo ritual at a hanging tree sounds perfectly normal doesn't it? It sounds normal to me but maybe that's because my family is cursed.

The voodouin whailed her misery and fell to the ground. "You will pay for this done this day!" The corpse swinging from the tree is all that remains of her lover.

This morning my sister Alex told me to stop at the "Witches Brew", "Just pick up a few things" she said. "Tetra will have everything ready for you, just hurry because we both needed to get on the road". My sister was right about Tetra and everything was ready. For a small town like ours in east Texas a witch was a big deal. I'm surprised she hasn't been burned at the stake already. I guess the locals are growing more tolerant. Maybe it's just me but I don't think I would ever set up shop as a witch in a redneck town. I had never been to her shop and was more than a little bit skeptical. I wondered what kind of weird crap I was going to have to pick up. I had visions of lizard's tongues and little hairy squirrels balls in tidy little jars lined up on shelves. My bad idea meter was pegged all the way on that one, but to each his own.

The shop was an old house with all the gingerbread and Victorian details painted bright shades of red, green, and purple. Annie was just as colorful but much younger and prettier than I had envisioned. I swear there wasn't a wart to be seen and she didn't even have a pointy hat. Tetra was wearing blue jeans with holes that came naturally, not the ones you pay $300 for in the mall. The t-shirt she wore was a tie dyed Joe's Crab Shack one and on her feet were flip-flops with a myriad of toe rings. I could commiserate with her unruly red hair escaping a French braid.

I looked around as Tetra finished a conversation with someone on the phone. As I browsed I noticed the beautiful jewelry and charms near the counter where the owner stood. The shop was full of work from local artists and I was sad to have just discovered such a jewel on the verge of my leaving town. Sometimes my sister is actually right, this place was cool. Tetra moved around the counter extending a hand in welcome. "You must be Kat? I can't tell you how much your sister talks about you and your artwork. If you ever want to leave some pieces here on consignment I would love it." She showed me through the shop and eventually ended up in a back room which was part of the living quarters. Alex had given her a list of everything we needed for the Voodoo ritual as well as a number of things she would take with her to Wyoming. I gathered up a box and Annie carried the other to my Jeep. I patted her 3 legged dog named Lucky and headed for the farm.

I rushed home, 65 in a 60 m.p.h. zone, I'm a real speed demon! I had a Voodoo ritual to perform on a creepy tree and I wanted to get it over with. Heading for the family farm for the last time I was anxious. My theory is that family is the original "F" word. The farm had been in our family for over 150 years. Alex and I decided to break the cycle and escape, sell it and never look back. We were heading our separate ways to find an end to the curse that pervaded our family history. As I drove home for the last time I wondered what we would find, if the curse could even be lifted.

The road was treacherous and I could count the spots where friends and family had missed curves, ate dirt, and hit trees. Rounding my favorite curve, the one where my neighbors' spittoon cup flew across the dash onto his snotty sister on our way to school. She had always been so mean to me. I know it wasn't polite but I cracked up laughing when that happened. The three "popular" people had crowded into the front seat leaving me alone

in the back like a dork. It must have been a Karma thing.
Sometimes life is sweet.

It was on that same curve that I spotted the cow. She was
standing in the road chewing her cud. I pulled up next to her and
leaned out the jeep to speak to her. No, that's not weird. I was
raised on a farm and I always talk to cows.

"What are you doing in the road? Yeah, like she was going
to answer. "Get back over there in your pasture!" She took a
step forward and looked at me. I thought I was going to have to
park and put her in myself when she just walked over and back
through the decrepit fence like she actually knew what I said to
her. Shaking my head, I drove on to the farm to finish packing.

When I got there Alex had her car attached to a U-Haul
truck and I had my Jeep and the trailer parked in the drive. We
finished packing and loading most of our stuff after a few rounds
of "I don't want it, you take it". There were way too many garish
objects to go around. Over a half a dozen generations of women
being raised by men equals ugly décor. Luckily my sister and I
liked different things so we didn't have to arm wrestle over
anything. My sister is all earth-mother witchy and I'm all Goth
meets Frida Khalo. We were twins but there was more than just a
difference in hair color between us. Alex has black hair to match
her dark depths and my unruly red hair mimics my carefree
approach to life.

We took a break and Alex took out the Black Sea Salt and
herbs while I gathered the Voodoo knife with the carved wooden
pirate sheath from my Wrangler. Alex had found the knife while
digging through resale shops five years earlier and we've fought
over it ever since.   With the items we needed in hand we headed
for our grandfather's old house. After he passed on we cleaned
out the house and were shocked by what we found. I was going
through a stack of photos when "it" dropped out of a pile. The
photo was small, black and white, old, and very disturbing. I got
a chill just looking at it.

There was a black man hanging from a tree and it was real,
he was real dead! There was a crowd around and the creepiest
thing was a little boy staring straight at the camera. They were

gathered around like it was a movie and all that was missing was the popcorn.

The young Voodoo priestess places the paper inside a poppet and stitches the little doll back together. Inside she has buried the ritual poem with her dark desires voiced along with the graveyard dirt and human hair. "Papa Legba hear my words true they be. Help me to make them pay that done us wrong."

I handed the photo to my sister and the shudder that shook her just reiterated my own feelings. She said when we were kids she had heard of a lynching but the adults clammed up when they saw her. We both looked at the picture and at the same time realized that we knew that tree.

It was the "creepy tree". The biggest, scariest looking tree on the property and we had always steered clear of it. We had constantly gotten a bad feeling about it. Others in our family had just claimed it was another weird "twin" thing.

Today we were going to try and lay the ghost of that tree to rest and hopefully rid ourselves of our "F"amily past. I had Apache tears in my pocket, otherwise known as obsidian to keep the dead at rest. Alex said, "Kat, we really need three people. Why don't we invoke Mom's spirit?"

I yelled, "No! We don't want her trapped here." We walked our circles, sprinkled the sea salt and herbs, buried the obsidian, and prepared to seal the bargain with blood. Of course I had forgotten to sharpen the knife and it was so dull it wouldn't draw blood. We kept half assed trying but in reality we were both chicken.

We didn't really know what we were doing but I had read the Anita Blake books so theoretically I knew how to bind the dead. We had to have blood to seal the deal. Alex is a witch and she knows this stuff. We had just never tried anything like this before. Finally Alex said, "wait." "I cut myself shaving this morning." She pulled her skirt aside and turned her leg to show a really nice slice.

"Jeez Alex were you trying to kill yourself?" She just ignored me and bent down to re-open the wound and squeezes a few drops of blood out. Alex wiped the blood on the blade and stabbed it into the ground. We did the salt circles and the words together

Leslie Brown

"With this steel I bind you to your grave, with this blood I bind you to your grave, and with this salt I bind you to your grave".

The dead Voudoin gasped as she felt the change coming. Inside her tomb she had the knowing that it would soon be over. Her lover's soul would be released and she could join him at the crossroads, but only if the curse was ended. Baron Samedi would lead her from this dark place.

The ritual at the tree was Ouija board creepy, like when you were a kid and managed to scare yourself playing with one of the stupid games.

After lingering hugs and tears we each left that haunted place heading in opposite directions to make new lives for ourselves. We had always existed with the curse but we were intent on finding a way to break it. Alex headed to Wyoming to search for answers among her Native American friends. I headed to the place where I felt at home, New Orleans.

I guess this is a good time to tell you who I am. My name is Kat, short for Katrina. Yeah, I know very funny. Well I had it long before that foul-breathed bitch came to town! New Orleans has always been my home of heart. Our mother had met our father there. She was searching for an end to the curse but was unsuccessful. I planned to take up where she left off sniffing out clues to the cure.

Our father told us of the curse when we were 12 years old. He had an old scrapbook filled with notes and letters. The first was a written diary by our great-great-great something Grandmother. In a nutshell it said that all the females in our family will die in childbirth. We will know true love briefly and conceive the night we lose our virginity. The only escape was through immortality. We grew up knowing this and had many generations before us as proof. The widows of our family had always passed on this knowledge to the children who were always female. My sister and I were the first twins. I was convinced that the hanging at the tree had something to do with the curse.

Alex thought that her friends could help but I believed the answer was in New Orleans. As far as we had researched that is where the curse began. I moved to New Orleans to find answers. That's how I ended up rescuing a vampire.

Chapter 2

When I arrived in the city I settled in a historic building on Royal Street that was supposedly haunted by a girl. No surprise there though, you can't throw a rock 3 feet in the Quarter without hitting a ghost. The story was that a beautiful girl had frozen to death on the roof. That didn't bother me because I always had good vibes around ghosts. They almost seem to like me. The house was expensive but I figured I might as well waste some of the money from the "F"amily farm. My family put the fun in dysfunctional. Imagine 7 generations of men raising females. I intended to use some of the family funds for my quest to find an end to the curse as well as start my own business. This building would give me a starting point. The structure had retail area below and living quarters in the second and third floors with roof access as well. I guess I could go up there and hang with the ghost. There was even a small courtyard with a fountain. It was just perfect for what I had in mind.

The house was typical of Creole architecture with the beautiful wrought iron balconies on the upper floors. I had inherited some humongous hanging plants with the place that I was sure to kill just with my presence but for now they looked lush and provided some privacy from the constant crowds passing by. The top floor had two adjoining rooms that would serve as a bedroom and studio as well as a luxurious bathroom with a gigantic claw footed tub.

The second floor housed a kitchen, living, and dining rooms with a half bath. The previous tenant had a teashop in the building years before Katrina. I painted the walls and re-finished the floors to bring out the beauty of the original wood. After the hurricane many established businesses closed and new ones like my own have taken their places.

For the first month I worked every day setting up the gallery and looking for help. Finally the right person came along, an artist named Skye willing to work for a small salary plus commission and a corner to sell her own work. Skye makes sculptures out of found objects and repurposed items. They are whimsical delicate things and I fell in love immediately. Her work is a great compliment to my own. I paint scenes from New Orleans with Mardi Gras revelers and Jazz musicians. I frame them with architectural pieces from junkyards and broken pieces from antique furniture that I find in junk shops and yard sales.

Skye creates delicate figures of fairies, nymphs, mermaids, and such with Mardi Gras attire. The redecorating and art displays were finished. The shop was perfect for opening night. The new sign out front told the name we had chosen, "Arti-Gras" sure to attract loads of loaded tourists with bulging wallets! The walls were filled with my paintings and various displays around the rooms were overflowing with Skye's sculptures. The caterers had delivered and set up everything and my sister had flown in for the opening. Everything was set up and ready but me. As usual I was scrambling at the last minute to get cleaned up and do something with my hair. Not a priority with me. I never worry about my hair and it is one flowing mass of red curls in contrast to Alex's jet-black straight hair. I had always wanted hair like hers, nothing too drastic just hair that you can actually comb.

When I came downstairs Alex was already greeting the first few guests and looked stunning in her slinky black dress. She smiled at me as I entered the room in my deep purple tuxedo. I have a severe allergy to dresses. Still I looked pretty good I thought. The suit was dressy and a sharp contrast to my usual duds. I prefer combat boots and camo. My riotous red curls were temporarily tamed into an elegant coiffure thanks to my patience.

The opening was just a blur of greetings and names I was hopeless to ever remember. Thank goodness for the guest book that Skye had thought of. The guests wound their way through the rooms and made a commendable dent in the champagne and buffet. I sold several large pieces and made appointments for nine commissions. Skye was giddy at the sales she had also made. She looked so cute tonight and reminded me of one of her fairies with her whimsical outfit. Usually she was dressed in pink and black Goth duds. Thanks to all their help it was a roaring success and I really owed Alex and Skye big time.

The day after the opening I took Alex on a tour of my favorite places. Alex only had a few days and most of our time had been spent getting ready for the opening. Now we took some time to relax. We went through the French Quarter and I pointed out many historical places like the Cornstalk Hotel, my favorite hotel in town. Later as we browsed the shops we toured the Voodoo Museum and I could tell it upset her a lot. "This place is just freaking creepy" Alex muttered in my ear as we moved from one room to another following the guide. "Aw, look at that cute snake" I said as we passed a glass case with a huge albino python inside. Alex hates snakes. "There is absolutely nothing cute about this place." Alex shuddered as she looked at the gator headed Papa Legba statue, a man with a gator head. Papa Legba is a sort of Voodoo god. "He's so cute; you might want to give up your abstinence sis." I nudged an elbow at Alex as I told her that. "Very funny, you first" she said. The Voodoo Museum was where I had learned a lot about the curse and about Voodoo. Papa Legba is a Loa or God of the religion Voodoo. Papa Legba is the guardian of the crossroads, basically a link between life and death.   All ceremonies begin and end with him. In the ceremonies offering of things like liquor and cigarettes are given.

From what I had learned the curse that had been laid on our family had to go through Papa Legba. Whoever had twisted that kind of a curse must have been powerful for it to last so long? We left the museum and headed down Dumaine to Royal and the gallery.

Alex and I finished our last evening together with a midnight cemetery tour. My friend is the honorary "Marie Laveau" and is the only guide in the city allowed to do cemetery tours after dark. We got on the streetcar at Canal and St. Charles. The hurricane ruined the new cars and the old streetcars were put back into service. The stops are on the wrong side of the cars because they are the opposite of the new ones. When you get on often you have to go around the cars and it's awkward especially near the riverfront. We managed to get on and rode down Canal in silence toward the cemetery. As we left the French Quarter I could imagine the water getting deeper and deeper like it did when the levees broke. The short ride ended at the cemetery and we were the only ones going that direction. The other passengers that rode to the end of the line were local workers rushing to catch the busses around the corner that would take them the rest of the way home. The corner where the streetcar ends is the tip of Odd

Fellows cemetery where we were meeting for the tour. The other tourist seemed to have either arrived earlier and we tagged onto the end of the line going inside. The tour was interesting and informative highlighting the history as well as telling a few ghost stories. The tour was a great end to my sister's visit. "If you find anything at all text me immediately" Alex told me as she stepped out of the Jeep to catch her plane. "Of course and the same goes for you" I said as she took off.

Chapter 3

My search for the cure seemed to be futile. It's hard to be subtle or even come across as sane when inquiring about Voodoo curses. When I questioned people about the curse I had to be very careful not to reveal anything about my actual curse. Part of the deal was that if anyone reveals the curse then it becomes accelerated, usually "accelerated" means something bad like pregnancy by rape. I so was not going there so I was extra paranoid. It had been three months since the opening and I had not found a single clue so far. When I wasn't manning the store I was out roaming the city searching for clues, sketching, and collecting broken antiques to artify. I take the broken antiques and architectural antiques and make my own frames.

Voodoo Joe's was where I was heading. The book I ordered had come in. The owner of the shop, Mama Jo-Jo is the local's favorite Voodoo practitioner. She runs Voodoo Joe's shop just as the women in her family have since before her grandmother could even remember. Mama Jo-Jo is the current honorary "Marie Laveau" and she has been helping me with research. Mama Jo-Jo is not at all what you would expect. She is in her early twenties, it's hard to tell exactly and I was certainly not going to ask. Jo looks more like a Rasta-Indie-Hippie convergence with her multi-colored dreadlocks and wild retro clothing.

One time when I asked her some questions about Voodoo she told me something I had not heard or read before. "When someone "twists" a curse that is hurtful and long lasting they have to pay dearly. To conjure through evil is a three-fold payback. Whatever the curse is comes back to them three times as bad. It takes a desperate person to get to the point where they don't care and do it anyway. Nearly all rituals are harmless or even made to do good. It's rare to see a dark curse." I thought about those words as I headed to the shop. How desperate could you get to cause decades of misery and death. What kind of misery was returned to the person who had conjured that curse?

I left my place on Royal, unlocking my bike from the street sign on the corner. I removed the seat while parked to discourage thieves which had worked so far. I put the seat back on and adjusted it. I think the number one actual crime in the French Quarter is bike theft. The day was still cool and I need to get out while I could stand it. I headed past Pirates Alley and turned left on St Philip. When I approached the Blacksmith's shop I slowed to take the corner on Bourbon Street. Voodoo Joe's was just ahead and I found a pole to lock my bike to. I removed the seat and put in my backpack with my sketching materials as I went inside. My eyes had to adjust to the dark shop and I nodded to the current derelict manning the cash register. It takes a creepy sort to want to work in a Voodoo shop. This newest guy was no exception. I saw Jo in the back talking to a customer and browsed the book section while waiting for her to finish. I picked up a small voodoo doll and read the tag which identified it as a love poppet.

The young priestess entered the cemetery where her lover was entombed. She kneels by the grave and removes the objects she has carried in the folds of her skirts. The little doll lay scattered amongst the coffee beans, cigar, bottle of rum, peanuts, and other items. The girl looks around uncertainly and places the doll inside the tomb. She places the other items around in a symbolic pattern and picks up the bottle of rum. Gesturing with her hands and uttering the words, "Papa Legba open the door." She knocks three times on the tomb. "I offer this to you in respect." She takes a deep swig of rum and spits it onto the tomb.

Mama JoJo inherited the Voodoo shop from her Grandmother who had recently passed away. I've spent a lot of time here researching under the guise of my art and have come to be friends with the quirky owner. I like her, she is not scary at all which is what I expected. Jo is actually learning a lot with me. When her grandmother passed away Jo was in training and not ready for the responsibilities thrust upon her at the time. My need for answers led me to Jo's shop which is a fountain of information. She told me about her Grandmother's house and all the strange things she grew up with. In the attic they even had a coffin and her Grandmother forbid her to go near it. Right before Jo's

Grandmother passed away she confided in her the secret of the coffin.

When Jo was finished with the customer she hugged me in a warm greeting. "I brought it" she said. "What?" "The coffin, come see it. I just know it will inspire you." We went to the back of the shop, past the ritual candles, gris-gris, and tarot cards and through the beaded curtains into the place where she usually does private readings.

"You gonna love dis" she whispered conspiratorially, her rainbow dreads bobbing as she walked. To one side a dusty velvet curtain was drawn aside with a tattered rope. Mama Jo-Jo waved me through the room and I squinted at the darkness. As my eyes adjusted I saw the coffin. The larger end was open and I could see a large object on the closed portion with chains twining all around and over the top. I looked at her in question with one eyebrow quirked up and she urged me on.

"Go ahead, take a look." I inched forward, not sure what to expect. As I got closer I saw him. It was a mummified corpse, covered in silver chains and crosses. "Gross."

"It's a vampire. I found him in the attic after my Gran passed."

I leaned over the open casket and looked a little closer. His bony fingers were clenched and his mouth was opened as if he had died in agony. Yeah, that sounds stupid because a vampire is already dead.

I turned back to her and asked, "Is this a prop for a haunted house or what?" She shook her head and her multi colored hair shook as she laughed.

"No, no, he is not a prop. He is a real vampire. My Gran told me on her deathbed. I must take care to not let him rise. I just figured why keep him hidden when I can charge $10 a head to see the vampire?"

She looked like the cat that fell into the cream standing there beside her vampire. I congratulated her on her business acumen and asked if I could stay and sketch him. She agreed and left me alone with the corpse. I pulled out my drawing book and pencil and made several quick sketches of the vampire. After a few minutes I put the sketches down and just looked at him.

Deja Voodoo   14

He was wearing a frock coat and a frilly shirt, typical vampire stuff. His hair was long and stringy dull gray. His skin had shrunken and stretched tight revealing a set of really impressive fangs yellowed with age. His claw like hands were crossed over his chest tipped with ragged sharp nails. He seemed so real that I had to check for myself. I tentatively touched the skin on one hand to feel the texture. I expected something like the hundred year old purses I had discarded at my Grandfather's place. Brittle and rough but was surprised to feel the tissue give a little as I pressed it. I thought it must be made of wax or rubber.

Feeling brave I had to test out his choppers. I prodded his upper lip up into an Elvis like curl and felt a fang. I tapped lightly with my fingernail. Boy I was gonna feel stupid if anyone saw me doing this. There was a reason they made that saying about curiosity and the cat. I was no exception to that rule.

I slid my finger down to feel the point and was surprised by how jagged it actually was. "Ow! That thing is really sharp," I said to myself. I pulled back and sucked on the bleeding finger. As I nursed my wound I watched the vampire's fangs where the drops of blood had spilled. It was like watching ants crawl on a leaf. The drops just traveled sideways to the point of his fang and disappeared. It was just creepy and I backed away quite disturbed by it. I grabbed my things and shoved them into my backpack to go. I waded through the heavy beaded curtain into the bookstore part of the Voodoo shop. There was a counter with a glass case an all different kinds of cigars displayed.

The Voudouin lit the cigar and blew smoke onto the tomb where the rum had darkened its' surface. "Papa Legba open the door I wish to speak to Baron Samedi." She wavers as the spirit fills her body.

As I left the shop I waved at Jo but rushed on to avoid any discussion. She was a good friend and was helping me immensely with the whole "curse" thing but she could eat up hours of your time just talking about ghosts and voodoo and I wasn't in the mood. I could get my book later. The vampire had kind of freaked me out enough.

Chapter 4

I dug in every crevice of my backpack twice searching for the key to unlock my bike and swore when it was exactly where I thought it should be. New Orleans was not the kind of place you needed to have a car. That was one of the reasons I fell in love with it. You can walk, bike, or take a streetcar and never use a car. Of course that didn't keep me from paying more each month to store my Jeep than a car payment. I may not drive it much here but I would feel like I lost a friend if I didn't keep it. You know, "it's a Jeep thing, you wouldn't understand." People who drive Wranglers are the only ones you see who always wave to each other.

I headed up Bourbon Street and stopped for lunch at Krystal, I just love those little burgers,   I hooked a right on Canal heading toward Odd Fellows Rest Cemetery. At the overpass I stopped to give a sack full of burgers to some homeless people staying under the bridge over Canal. I had planned to meet some other volunteers to work on the restoration of a tomb there and thanks to the vampire I was running late. I pumped hard on the pedals and it felt good eating up some of the nervous energy from earlier. I parked by the Herb shop and locked my bike to a pole noting where I put my keys this time.

The gate was unlocked and I eased it open to let myself inside. This was the side entrance and the nearest corner towards town. Odd Fellows is built on a small plot of land shaped like a triangle. If you view it from the sky it looks like a pyramid with a Celtic cross through it. The center has a mound where Brother Dunlop, one of the designers of the cemetery is buried. When it was opened in 1849 there was a huge Jazz funeral with the first burials of Odd Fellows being relocated from other cemeteries. They were transported in circus wagons pulled by matching white horses. Just the thought of such a ludicrous spectacle makes me smile.

The first time I came to this cemetery was on a spooky midnight tour and I fell in love with it instantly. Now I volunteer to help preserve the deteriorating tombs and clean the weeds out.

I walked up the aisle to the center and headed for Daniel's grave. He had a nice little spot with a beautiful tree and fence around it but the tree was dislodging everything. It had grown so large part of the fence was embedded into the tree. The tomb was crumbling and had holes in it as well.

Daniel died as a little boy probably during the epidemics that swept the area killing thousands. We had a psychic come read him and she said he had been crippled and picked on as a child. He often throws acorns down from his tree and to placate him we bring Lego's, matchbox cars, Mardi Gras beads, and such.

One time I brought Skye to see his grave and he made contact with me. We were locked in the cemetery alone and I had walked ahead to place some sea shells on the ledge of Daniels fence. I turned back and called to Skye to come see. When she joined me I turned back to look and the sea shells were gone. They had been replaced by a gold doubloon like what people throw at Mardi Gras. It freaked us out and we both ran off like a couple of sissies.

Half way back to the house we looked at each other and said at the same time "were we supposed to keep it?" I went back the next day and apologized for being so stupid. I told him I didn't mean to offend him that it just scared me. I thought, maybe he feels the same way with people bringing him stuff. I quit bringing him things and just talk to him now.

Everyone was already there and busy working when I showed up. Robert just looked at his watch and gave me a smirk. He had wanted to start later but I insisted on an earlier time. We were moving the fence out some to accommodate the tree and had already repaired his tomb. The work seemed endless, so many of the tombs are abandoned with no perpetual care or families to keep them up. I was making it my mission in life to help as much as I could. Ten percent of every sale in my shop went into restoration and we were planning an auction fundraiser and masquerade ball. I noticed a series of three x's drawn in chalk on one tomb and went over to clean it off.

The girl's cheeks were streaked with tears as she begged for help. "Please do this thing I ask." The Baron's voice echoes inside her head. "There will be a price to pay. Your soul will stay in the crossroads until the curse is untwisted." She shakes her

Leslie Brown   17

head acknowledging the fate and crawls inside the tomb with the shell that was her lover, a small price to pay for his vengeance.

After a couple of hours there I returned home to clean up and put in a few hours in the store. Skye had a hot date and probably needed to get a new tattoo in that honor so I was it for tonight. We only stayed open until 8 p.m. so it was only a couple of hours. I opened the door to relieve her and saw she was busy working on cleaning the shelves that held her sculptures. She was just arranging a purple faerie when she saw me. "Dude I am so ready to get outta here. I have so much to do. Can I go now?" Her sentences ran into each other and I didn't even get to respond before she grabbed her purse and flew out the door. "Sure, don't worry. I can handle all of this by myself," I said as I straightened the faerie which had fallen over onto its side. For the next several hours I paced the gallery floors anxiously, even a few hours felt like days though when I was itching to get into my studio and paint. A few customers came in, mostly tire kickers. When the last one left a few minutes before eight I followed her to the door and flipped the closed sign around while locking the door and setting the alarm.

Chapter 5

The vampire had been on my mind all day and I had been having visions of what he must have looked like before, or if he had been real. I went upstairs and changed yet again to get ready to paint. I didn't so much as change but threw off my shirt, bra, and dirty jeans and threw on a humongous old t-shirt on. It was covered in paint and soft and warm and I just like it. Underneath the paint you can still read the saying "Don't make me go voodoo on your ass" in big white letters.

I visualized the vampire and painted him as I had imagined. I worked furiously with the life size portrait until well past 3 a.m. when I finally fell into bed exhausted. It must have been shortly after that I had a dream, it felt real though just kind of fuzzy, like a cold medicine induced hallucination of sorts. In the dream my window was open and the wind was whipping the curtain around. I looked at the billowing material and that is where he emerged. I knew him immediately. It was the vampire, the one from Voodoo Joe's. Luckily my mind had brought him back to his drop dead gorgeous former self. This was my dream and he could be as cute as I wanted him to be. The wrinkled skin was replaced with carved marble abs framed in the requisite billowing white shirt that everyone knows vampires always wear. His black slacks were low on his hips and the button was undone. I thought, "Damn I have good dreams, please don't let the alarm ring".

He came forward and slithered onto the bed and above me. It was like he was hovering, I couldn't feel his weight pressing into my body. Damn the bad luck. His long black hair fell in a shadow over his eyes so that I couldn't see what color they were. Somehow I knew they were green like my own. I shivered as he kissed me. That's more like it I thought. This was not a gentle kiss but a deep ravaging that robbed me of my breath and my senses.

Vaguely I remember thinking thank God this is a dream. I'm not supposed to be doing this. My life depends on it. I reveled in the feel of his lips and his tongue rasping my ear and raged internally. I really should stop this. If I have sex I get pregnant. No negotiation, no birth control, no options. The curse decrees that I will die in childbirth and my daughter will grow up without a mother. That's why I had never dated. I have always been very careful to keep temptation at bay. Dreams are different though. They aren't real.

I let myself enjoy this little bit of life that I was forced to miss out on. His lips were strong and he nipped and bit his way down my neck as his hands drug my t-shirt up. I felt down his chest with my fingertips and nails lightly digging in. He was absolutely scrumptious. His hands grasped my rear and lifted me to rub against his swollen erection. We writhed back and forth causing heat with the friction. A moan escaped me when the piercing shrill of the alarm swept him from my arms.

"Damn it! That was just getting good!" I raged and forced my eyes closed. Maybe I could bring the dream back. I imagined how it had felt but it was no good. I was awake and the dream had fled. Shit, shit, shit!

Oh well, it was good while it lasted. I got up, showered, and got dressed for my usual day in the store. Before going downstairs I went to the top floor studio to see the painting I had done the night before. I could barely remember what I had done.

There it was on the easel. It was stunning, a perfect image of the man from my dreams with haunting green eyes. I didn't remember finishing it let alone building a frame for it but there it was. I don't even know why I did it. I don't do portraits. I don't like painting people. It was so odd and out of place with my other work. I carried it downstairs and set it on another easel in the main gallery.

Chapter 6

The gallery did not open for a couple of hours but I needed to do some paperwork and get some breakfast. Arg! I hate doing the boring stuff, but I am sure that is just me. Other people must love to balance books and do inventory. Why else would anyone become an accountant? I left the shop heading down Royal Street and through Pirates Alley towards the river, and past Jackson Square to Café Du Monde. The place has the best beignets and is a favorite of locals and tourists alike. I was painfully addicted to the Beignets and chicory coffee. You just have to be careful and don't wear black. There's nothing like a powdered sugar infestation to kill your Goth wardrobe. Just bad for the image I guess. I know Skye would never be caught dead here. I blissfully consumed a plate of doughnuts and finished my coffee before returning to open the shop. Starbucks my ass!

It was Saturday and the crowds would be milling soon. The open sign was already out and I could see Skye looking at the portrait I had painted the night before. She barely glanced at me as I entered and headed for my desk. After a while she came over and just gushed.

"I am in L-O-V-E! When did you do it? Is it for sale? I didn't know you did portraits."

When she took a breath I answered patiently, "What's new, last night, no, and no, to answer all of your questions". Skye had a habit of bombarding me with sentences like raid fire ammunition from a semi automatic rifle.

She turned back to it and I smiled at her reaction. You had to love her. She was this quirky little thing, all Barbie gone Goth. Picture Abby on the T.V. show N.C.I.S. crossed with a Saints cheerleader. "I'm glad you like it. He just poped into my imagination somehow."

I was pleased by her reaction. I guess I do portraits after all. She kept staring at it all day and I had to wait on most of the customers. I was going to have to do something with that thing. It wasn't doing much for my nerves either. I kept thinking of the dream and turned red every time Skye saw me looking at it. After a while she came over and sat on my desk with her purple New Rock boots clicking furiously.

"What gives?" She was ready to grill me. I knew it was coming and still didn't have my mind made up on what to say yet.

I just told her I had a great erotic dream and he was a figment of my imagination. I didn't tell her about Voodoo Joes. Somehow I felt protective towards him. I kept thinking about it all day and when we finally closed shop I got out of my dress clothes, threw on my jeans and raced over to see him again. The Voodoo shop kept Bourbon Street hours so they were still open. On the way over I dodged the early crowds as I rushed in the door. During the day I had convinced myself that I was just crazy. There was no way he was real. I had been researching too much voodoo mumbo jumbo and in the city of ghosts I was getting loopy.

Lack of sex could also have something to do with it. For Pete's sake I was 26 and still a virgin. That pesky death curse can really be a great endorsement for abstinence. It's no wonder the women in my family gave in. At least they had 9 months of bliss before dying.

With that thought I nodded to the clerk and parted the beaded curtain to view the vampire once again. The hallway leading into the alcove that held the coffin was dim and the walls were covered with dusty art and Voodoo items including an altar to Papa Legba.

The tomb was putrid with the decaying body of her lover but she ignored that and crawled inside on the lower level. She was trading her life and soul to twist the curse for revenge. "Baron Samedi guide me to the crossroads where I must be. Papa Legba seal this tomb, take my bones and soul to keep, my curse to feed." The tomb facing slid back into place.

I set my backpack down and moved closer. Was it my imagination or did his skin seem fuller around his mouth? It was. I distinctly remember it being more shrunken up. I must really be losing it. I took out my camera and snapped off a few shots. Then I sat down and started sketching him.

The coffin was quite beautiful with ornate patterns carved in to a rich dark wood. Nothing like modern coffins with their

Deja Voodoo

gleaming metallic finishes. This one looked like someone had lovingly carved it for someone important. The details were amazing. I could just imagine me trying something like that. I would have it almost finished and wham! I would slip and chop off something important. I guess David was lucky Michelangelo had steady fingers. I laughed thinking about "The Goonies" when the kid knocked over and broke the replica of David's penis and the other kid said, "that was my Mom's favorite part."

I must be getting tired; my thoughts were getting goofy so I put my sketchbook away. I had drawn the vampire in detail and had pictures to show for proof. I would come back in a few days and compare them to prove that my imagination was just working overtime. He could not be real. This time I was cautious but again I ran my finger over the fangs and quickly pierced the skin. I felt the blood leaving my body and before I lost all thought I jerked my hand away and quickly left.

Chapter 7

The next several days I tried to put the vampire out of my mind as I spent all my spare time researching to find an answer to the mystery of my family's curse. Each night though he visited and the dreams became more real. It was hard to concentrate during the day I knew from the notes and information left by my ancestors that the curse had originated in New Orleans during the reign of Marie Laveau. The curse was from a lesser known Voodoo practitioner possibly trained under Marie sometime between 1850 and 1860.

From the pieces I had put together the man hanged at "the tree" was the lover of that woman. Presumably the curse was payback for his death. I poured over the scraps of paper and notes written by generations of women doomed to die young. Her great great something grandmother Catriona seemed to be the beginning of it all. There had to be a way out. There was a poem on faded paper in the scrapbook written by the priestess and given to Catriona along with a gris gris dated 1858. The gris gris presumably held the curse. It was a bag filled with what my great-something-grandmother described in her journal as something a cat hacked up. A hairball with teeth along with some bones and odd dust, feathers, and unidentifiable stuff. The poem was attached to the gris gris bag.

> Deaths embrace, cloying limbs held,
> Love beyond my grasp.
> Her treachery revealed,
> Endless misery.
> For taking him she shall pay,
> Satisfaction mortal agony.
> True love ends in tragedy,
> Death with every new life bring.
> Only to begin again,
> Generations left to pay,
> Unspeakable unjustice done.
> No mothers love to know,
> Every female child to alone.
> Life conceived at the time,

Of innocence lost.
Sealed lips to keep you safe,
Suffer more for secrets revealed.
Pay this debt forevermore,
'Immortal release, cursed no more.

Generation after generation of my family has lived the curse. Each mother dies in childbirth leaving a daughter behind to carry on the legacy. We aren't allowed to tell anyone about it or the curse could worsen. Over the generations we have learned more through human trial and error. Birth control does not work. I'm living proof, or shall I say we. My grandmother just tried to abstain and ended up being raped. There was no way to fight it.

Catriona slides into bed satisfied that her father has punished that stupid servant and his evil lover. How dare they try and trick her. She paid a high price for them to secure her heart's desire but it failed. They were just fakes. The man was hanged for stealing and the woman had been flogged and sent back to her family in tatters. "Served them right." She mumbled to herself as she snuggled up to the pillow. Her hand felt something and she jerked back tossing the pillow aside to reveal what was hidden underneath.

I re-read the poem for the millionth time when the words registered with me. 'Immortal release, cursed no more- that was it! If I was immortal I could not die. That had to be it. O.K. now I just need to figure out how to achieve my immorality. With that in mind I pulled out my sketches of the vampire and compared them to the painting I had made. There was no doubt they were one and the same. He was a little crispy in my sketches but the same no doubt. I thought just maybe the answer was right before me.

Chapter 8

I gathered up my sketches and ran out to see for myself if he was real. I sped through the quarter dodging drunken tourists and locals. It was a busy day in the French Quarter. Jo was not at the shop but the guy behind the counter was used to me and I went right back. Throwing my stuff down in the corner I leaned over the coffin to look closely. Shit! His lips were drawn back again! The photos I had taken were defective, but my sketches were proof. It was not my imagination. I steeled myself and brought my hand up to his mouth. Quickly I impaled my index finger on one his very sharp fangs. I intended to find out for sure. He just needed more blood. I would have to stick it out. Almost immediately I could feel the pull of my blood running down through my veins and pooling at my fingertip. The blood disappeared into his fang.

After a few minutes I started feeling dizzy and I blinked trying to clear the cobwebs from my mind. All I could see was him, stalking towards my bed and how good it felt kissing him. I kept thinking there was something I needed to remember. Sluggishly I struggled to push the memory out of my mind. I opened my eyes and looked at him. How long had I stood there with him draining me? His flesh had filled out considerably and he was looking very much more alive. I jerked my hand away and stumbled backwards, falling flat on my ass.

I couldn't believe I had done that. It was so stupid. He could have drained me like a keg at a frat party. I stood up and approached him more cautiously. He had definitely livened up a bit. I was leery of him but I was not afraid. My courage was kind of stupid if you think of it. He was a real vampire. He could have killed me I reasoned in my mind, but probably not in his weakened state. I left with thoughts heavy in my head, working on a plan.

I went home and again took up my paintbrushes until the early hours of the morning. I created yet another portrait of what he must have looked like before being trapped in that cross draped prison. I wondered what he must have done to end up there. That night as I slept he came to me again in my dreams.

Deja Voodoo

It was so much more real than a dream. I opened my eyes to see him standing before me. His eyes were sparkling green just as I had painted them. He moved closer, predatory like a leopard stalking its prey. This wasn't real, it was just a dream. It was just my mind playing tricks. I relaxed with the security that this was not real and therefore didn't count.

He lay on the bed next to me without so much as the tiniest movement. If he was real I would have felt the bed sinking as he settled next to me. I lay my hand upon his alabaster chest feeling the muscles under his skin shiver beneath my trailing fingers. He felt real but in my head he spoke. "You have given me the energy to travel on a metaphysical level." "Oh," I said out loud, unsure if he could read my thoughts. "Yes, I can", he said again in my mind. This could be bad I thought. This dream was turning very weird. I will have to be very careful or he will find out, I thought. "Find out what?" He asked again inside my head. I was in deep shit. I quickly changed my thoughts and he responded well to my prompting.

As far as I was concerned I might as well enjoy my hallucination or whatever this was. I kissed him, tongue delving and exploring his mouth, teeth, and fangs. Never before had I allowed myself this temptation. My life depended on it. His lips were like juicy strawberries and I was ravenous. His hands burrowed under my t-shirt and drove it up to reveal my breasts. He licked and kissed his way along my belly, taking a moment to flick the little belly button ring I wore. The tiny moon and stars twinkled as I laughed at his tickling tongue. I shivered as he expertly took one nipple with his lips and tongue. His hands roved over every inch of my body. He cupped me from inside my underwear and that was enough to bring me over the edge and back to my senses. I sat up and pushed him away and he disappeared before my eyes.

"Whoa!" That was entirely too strange. I pulled my shirt down and hugged my pillow towards me.

Catriona poked at the disgusting ball of cloth and it rolled off the bed. She screamed and the chambermaid came inside to see what was wrong now. She looked at the bundle on the floor and crossed herself. "That be bad Voodoo." She skirted around the thing and went to her mistress grabbing her arm to lead

Catriona out of the room. "Did you touch it?" Catriona nodded in assent. "That's a gris gris, very bad. I tol' you not to mess wit' those people. Now look what you done brung to yourself."
This was going way too fast. I needed to think. I needed to talk to Alex. I reached for my cell phone and pushed the "1" and listened to the ringing. "Kat" she asked", what's wrong?"
I spilled my guts and told her everything that had happened since the opening. "I think that he is a real vampire. He definitely changed. I didn't just hallucinate it. I've been back several times each time I gave him some of my blood and he is improving."

"It makes sense," Alex said. "If he is a vampire he could turn you and then you would be immortal just like that poem says. It's got to be the answer."

"He seems so real when I am sleeping he is always there in my dreams.

"Vampires are the ultimate immortal" she said. "You have to get him to turn you." She was very insistent and I noticed a strange quality to her voice. "What's wrong?" I asked her. The other end of the line went silent and I waited getting more and more nervous. "Spit it out" I prompted her again.

"I'm pregnant!" Alex blurted out and burst into sobs. "I didn't mean to but he was there and I was there and it just happened. I'm scared. I love him but there is more at stake than he knows and I can't tell him." I calmed her down and assured her that I would not let it get to that point. It had happened two days ago and that gave me almost nine months to fix this.

Chapter 9

The next morning with renewed determination I began putting my plan into motion. I went to Voodoo Joe's, not to see the vampire, because I could feel him. I knew he could feel me too. I went to see Jo. I asked her some general questions about voodoo and curses on the pretext of artistic research.

"If a person put a curse on someone else that could only be broken through immortality," I asked, "what did that mean?" She eyed me up and down and said: "that's a very tricky curse to twist. I suppose it could mean quite a few different things." " What about vampirism?" I asked her, "your vampire in the back for instance. If he was real he would be immortal, right?"

" What makes you think he ain't real? He's as real as you and me. There's a price for immortality and it might not be worth it. Just ask him, he's alive but he ain't living!" Jo worked very hard to look like a "Voodoo Queen" but it was hard to take her seriously since I knew her so well and she did not look intimidating. She wore a long skirt made of flimsy fabric that moved with her body. The black blouse she wore billowed and exposed a great deal of cleavage. She knew her business though. Jo had come from a long line of Voodoo practitioners. The shop was named after her great grandfather Joe. She advised me to be very careful. "Immortality comes at a great price. Don't go messin' around in the realm of the undead".

With that disturbing conversation I left more confused than ever. I don't know who trapped the vampire in that coffin but I just don't feel he deserved it. He doesn't feel evil to me. On the contrary, I get a feeling of compassion and sadness. Maybe if I release him he will be grateful enough to help me. With that thought I set out to release the vampire.

Giving him my blood was out of the question. I could tell already that what I had given him strengthened a bond between us. I just did not want to go too far. I didn't need my mind clouded. Alex's life depended on it. I was damned if I was going to let one more generation grow up motherless. The first problem was how to get my hands on some human blood since I wasn't offering any. It's so white trash to put out on the first date anyway.

With the help of a few of Skye's friends that knew enough to not ask questions I was able to get a shipment of freshly donated blood that managed to "fall off" a shipping truck. I transferred it to my hydra pack that I used when bike riding. Hopefully the 2 gallon reservoir would be enough to give the vampire strength to rise. I slipped it on my back and headed to Voodoo Joe's. The same punk worked the counter as before. I could see he was selling drugs on the side as usual from the way the customer twitched and looked nervous. Jo really needed to get rid of that guy he reeked of bad news. I skirted a wide path around them and I went straight back.

The heavy curtains clanked against the wall as I passed through them into the dark hallway. I saw a painting of Marie Laveau and paused to contemplate what kind of magic a person could conjure to create a curse like this. In the painting her face was turned upwards and her hands were lifted holding a huge snake in the air. There were people circling her and the fire she stood by. They danced to the invisible beat of a drum and one face in the crowd stood out. The girl faced the view staring straight out as if she could see you watching that private ceremony. It was very unsettling.

Catriona dismissed the little bundle holding the cursed poem as foolish. She had more important things to worry about. The man she loved had married another and she had to figure out a way to get him back. She had slipped out of the house and followed the banquette careful to keep her skirts out of the filthy streets. She hated New Orleans and would be glad when she would be able to settle back in Texas with Julien. She let herself into his office and found him alone. He smiled in greeting and held out his arms.

"I thought you wouldn't forgive me. I had to marry her. You know my business is bankrupt without her family fortune." "I realize that now. You did what you had to do." She came around the desk and they embraced. His kisses heated her so it was like she had no control. She knew it was wrong but she had to have him. She would deal with his wife later.

Deja Voodoo

I put the pack down and as quietly as possible removed the crosses and silver chains draped across the coffin. The big one on top was extremely heavy and it took a while to move it. Luckily the Bourbon street noise drowned out most of my own. I settled the hydra pack in the coffin and pressed the suction hose to his lips.

"Drink" I urged him. When I saw the blood flowing I left him there. I walked away as if nothing had happened. Worry filled my mind and numbed my bones. I walked for what felt like hours but must have only been minutes. When I took my bearings I realized I was at St. Charles Avenue near Canal Street. I saw the streetcar approaching and automatically reached for my pass to board. I rode down St. Charles past the beautiful Garden District to Audubon Park and exited there. As I walked the path shrouded in huge trees at midnight I thought this wasn't the safest thing to do but I needed fresh air, I needed to think. I had walked the entire loop to the zoo and back when I decided to head home.

I was walking back towards St. Charles Avenue when I felt his presence. My heartbeat sped up. I'm not sure if it was fear or anticipation. This was it, he was going to bite me, and I would become immortal. I held my breath waiting for death to come claim me. His arms encircled me just right. I relaxed back into them, unable to see but knowing it was him. I was determined to be brave. From this point there would be no turning back, I had made my decision. I tilted my head to reveal my long neck. I had put my hair up in anticipation. His hands wrapped around my waist. I could feel his breath on my neck.

"Make me like you" I asked.

He released me so suddenly I stumbled forward and had to catch my balance. I faced him with accusation in my eyes.

"You owe me!" He backed a step away from me and I advanced on him. I don't know where I got the nerve but I just snapped. Rushing forward I jabbed him in the chest with my index finger and said: "I let you out of that box so that you would help me." I pulled back my finger realizing how ludicrous it seemed. He reached for me and pulled me into his steely arms. This kiss was not like before in my dreams. It was harsh and real. I fought him at first but soon turned tactics and returned his kiss with my own aggression. Big mistake. I thought it would make him mad but it just made me frustrated. I wanted this so badly but it had to be on my terms. The curse had to be broken, I had to die a virgin and become immortal. Yeah sometimes life sucks but apparently my vampire wouldn't.

He let me go and stood there arms crossed trying to figure me out. He probably thought I was insane. Who could possibly release a vampire and ask them to kill them? This was not going well at all. I held my hand out and introduced myself.

"Let's start this over. Hello, I'm Kat, short for Katrina." I didn't bother with the hurricane reference- he probably didn't know about it. It looked like he had been in that coffin for decades at least. He slowly grasped my hand and for the first time I heard him speak.

"I'm Tarik" he said. We shook hands briefly and retreated a pace. I guess we both needed space.

"O.K. so why don't you want to make me a vampire?" I asked as I watched him. I thought my painting looked pretty good but it was nothing compared to the real thing. This guy was major eye candy.

"Well you don't waste time on small talk. That's fair enough. What do you know about being a vampire?"

"I know enough" I said. "A vampire sucks you dry and gives you his or her blood, therefore turning you into a vampire. You die and become immortal. You drink blood, sleep in a coffin, and need SPF 666."

He snorted. "Quite the little wise ass I see. What, by the way is SPF?" I told him it was sunscreen, I guess he had been in lockdown for quite a while. He growled at me, "let me tell you, being a vampire is unbearable! I didn't ask for this and I wouldn't wish it on my worst enemy. I swore never to turn another human again! Just go home and forget about becoming a vampire. Tomorrow's headlines should be enough to convince you!" With that he flashed off so fast it whipped my hair around. Again? I wondered what that meant.

I stuck my tongue out at him anyway and stomped off to the streetcar. The next morning I realized what he meant as I sipped my coffee at Café Du Monde and read the Times-Picayune.

The headline read: "Carnage found at Voodoo Joe's." Apparently the store clerk and two customers were found shortly after midnight last night with their throats ripped out. The clerk was the zit faced punk rocker that I had just left alone with a vampire. Oh shit, this was my fault. I should have stayed. He was a scumbag but he didn't deserve to die. I should have given him more blood. It's my fault they're dead. These thoughts raced through my head all day.

I went by Voodoo Joes to give my condolences to Mama Jo Jo. The shop was already open, death waits for no one, and the city never stops. Jo was behind the counter and she glared at me accusingly and said:

"I hope you know what you're doing. I have a missing money maker and 3 dead cause of it." I guess the hydra pack gave me away. She turned her back on me and I left.

She was right it was my fault. I should have planned better. Later that night as I slept fitfully he came to my window. I woke to his presence knowing it was him like you know what size shoe you wear. There is no question it's a size 10 and you just know it. I knew it because there were never any shoes in my size at the stores. I looked up at him and couldn't help but appreciate his perfection. It looked like my size ten was here to confront me.

"It wasn't your fault. It was my fault you killed those people. You wouldn't have done it if I had planned better."

In two steps he was in my face. "You had nothing to do with it. I killed them. I'm a vampire, it's what I do. What makes you think I won't just kill you too?"

I made a little O with my mouth and inhaled. "You just wouldn't" I stammered. "You don't have to kill to live. You can always find willing and deserving donors." I stated flatly. "The child predator web sites alone can provide you with meals indefinitely."

He looked at me and asked, "what's a web site?"

I didn't expect that and just laughed as I asked "how long were you in that coffin?"

"Many, many years and I have much to catch up on." With that he reached for me and kissed down my neck. I melted into the desire for an instance before I pulled back reluctantly.

"I can't do this. I want you but not like this. You have to help me. I need to become immortal. I can't tell you why it is so important but it is. I saved you. You save me. I know it won't be all great but I can accept that. Until then I am off limits."

"What the hell is wrong with you!" he yelled. I'm immortal but I am dead every day. I kill people to stay alive. I have no soul!" He pulled me up and out of the bed and ordered me to get dressed. I threw on some jeans and pulled a sweatshirt over my t-shirt. I slipped into some Keds and he towed me down the stairs and out onto Royal street. We walked silently through the streets and through an unlocked courtyard. The window was open and inside I could see a sleeping child.
"Do you want to watch me drain the life from her?" He whispered in my ear sending a shiver down my spine.

I glared at him and smacked him on the back of the head before I thought about it. He glared at me in challenge and I nodded upward. He followed my gaze to the second floor where we could see a man beating his wife, girlfriend, whatever.

"He looks more like a satisfying meal I whispered." I held my hand out to urge him on and he scaled the railing quickly ascending the balcony. The woman ran into the next room crying and the ass hole came out for a smoke. I watched as Tarik drained him.

The man slid to the floor and Tarik bounced over the balcony to land squarely in front of me in a crouching position.

"He's not dead. I can hear his breathing." I pointed out the fact smugly. "See you don't have to kill." I grabbed his hand and gave him a tug to his feet. We walked back in silence.

A few nights later he returned to my bedroom. I was so sleepy I didn't wake up fully until I felt his hand on my bare skin. I was naked and he was slathering my belly with his wicked tongue. His skin felt tantalizingly cool against mine which had become very hot. My hands were twined in his waist length blue black hair. Ten more seconds and I would have impaled myself on him.

"Damn it!" I yelled, "what the hell are you doing? I told you my terms! It's not fair to sneak up on me like that!" He grinned up at me and rolled onto his side revealing the fact that he too was nude and very happy to pose for me.

"I think I can persuade you" he said as he ran one finger down my side. My mouth went dry and I devoured him with my eyes. Is this what Eve felt like in the Garden? Just one little bite? I was in deep shit!

I gracefully skittered backwards and fell flat on my ass in a heap of sheets. Wrapping them around me I pointed to the window.

"Get out!" He stretched lazily like a cat and wagged his "tail" at me. This meant war! What an ass! Literally and figuratively. Two can play at that game I decided. I stood and I dropped my sheet. Standing there completely naked I just sauntered off to the shower.

He just laughed and said: "make it a cold one!" He was gone when I got out.

Chapter 10

The days drug by slowly and the nights ended too soon. I tried each night to make Tarik agree to turn me. We argued and flirted and teased each other. He thought he could have me without giving me what I wanted. Apparently he had been dead way too long. Women had gotten far more stubborn in the days he had been locked in his coffin. Days became weeks and weeks became months and time was running out.

One night when he came to my bedroom I was ready for him. I had been out shopping with a friend and bought the perfect little sexy dominatrix outfit with 6 inch heels and a whip. If I couldn't seduce him into giving in I just might beat him!

He came through the floor to ceiling window like usual but stopped dead in his tracks. No pun intended. I was artfully posed by the tall posts of the antique bed. He growled and reached for me in one sweeping movement. He bit into my neck and I was flooded with relief. It felt so good! I would save my sister and myself.

Suddenly he pulled free of me and threw me against the bed.

"No! I won't do this!" He raged and paced like a caged animal. Tears streamed down my face as it all seemed hopeless. He would never give in.

"Do you know why I was trapped in that coffin? He growled at me through clenched teeth.

"My own brother put me there." He ran his hands down through his long hair as he paced furiously.

"Thinking I was doing him a favor I gave him this dark gift! He hated me for it and swore revenge. That's why I have been locked away for so many years."

I stared in silent misery as he told the story.

"My brother was so happy. He was married and had two beautiful children but when they were killed he became a shell of a man. I thought I could save him, but all I have done is prolong his misery. I deserve what he did to me."

Tarik stopped pacing and reached for my hands to help me sit up. I asked, "I am sure you brother has come to terms with this by now. Maybe you should talk to him."

"Ha! My brother has come to terms with his lifestyle! He revels in it now. He has not seen me but I have seen him. He is a monster. He runs this city from his dark world. All the other monsters look up to him. He has taken my place and is twisting the power to sut his own needs. No, Viktor is blissfully happy now but he is not the same and it is my fault."

"I'm sure Viktor has forgiven you," I consoled him. "This doesn't change anything though. I still want you to turn me. Time is running out for me and if you can't help me I will have to find someone who will. Perhaps you brother will oblige?"

"Stay away from my brother! Viktor doesn't know I am out and I want it to stay that way. Tarik took up pacing the small room again.

"I can't explain this to you. You just have to trust me, there is no other way. I want to be with you but it has to be as a vampire or not at all. If you aren't here to do this then just leave."

I turned away so that I did not have to see the rejection I knew was coming. Tarik's footsteps told me the answer. He was leaving.

Chapter 11

Time was truly running out. Alex was several months
along now and I was nowhere nearer to being immortal than when
I had arrived in New Orleans. I spoke to Alex by phone "he just
won't do it. I have no other choice I am going to see his brother."
I had done some research with Skye's help and found out that
Viktor owned a Goth club in town. Skye frequents it and had even
seen him before. She gushed about how hot he was ever since
she heard I wanted to meet him.

"Are you going to paint his picture too?"

"No, I have important business with him. A family matter."

*Catriona was lying in bed sweat pouring from her brow as
she struggled to give birth. Her last thought was for the curse,
surely it was just mumbo jumbo. The baby girl cried out in
protest as Catriona's heart stopped beating.*

*At the crossroads the priestess smiles and joins hands with
the Baron.*

We planned to go to Club Morte and Skye had taken me
out shopping for the perfect Goth outfit. I got some New Rock
boots but mine were black with purple flames. My skull stockings
were topped with a short, short skirt and shirt with a girly skull on
front. My hair was no problem, it had a mind of its own, and I just
let it go wild and free dangling down my back. I topped it off with
my leather Lucky 13 jacket and we were off.

Club Morte was not in the French Quarter but down by the
river in an old shipping warehouse. From the outside the only clue
it was a club was the many cars and the intense beat of the music.
We entered after being frisked presumably for weapons. More
likely for silver crosses and holy water squirt guns. The place was
packed from head to toe with sweating young Goths. The music
was live but I didn't know the band but Skye was in L-O-V-E with
the drummer. Of course he had yet to realize that she existed.
I'm sure by the end of the night she would find a way to let him
know. As expected she ditched me in 10 seconds or less. That

was fine with me. I had business to attend to and it was not anything she needed to be involved in.

I headed for the bar and after a few minutes finally got the girl tending bar to notice me. I handed her a 20 and asked where Viktor was. She snatched the 20 and then told me that if Viktor wanted me to know where he was he would find me. What the hell was that supposed to mean?

I wandered around and fended off the horny young men that were buzzing around like flies. I was in search of the ladies room when I spotted him. He didn't look anything like Tarik but I knew. He had a stillness that just screamed undead. His hair was three shades of brown from reddish to blondish in an uneven cut. It fell over his eyes but what I could see was stunning. They were a golden color like a lion and just as wary. He had a scrumptious Van Dyke goatee. His eyebrows were pierced as well as his nipples. He wore no shirt and dark russet leather pants with a matching long duster. No wonder Skye raved, he was yummy.

He approached me and spoke. "What could a prominent artist like you need to see a nefarious rake like me for?" His eyes stripped away the costume and saw through me instantly." I had heard his fingers were in every pie in town but how did he know about me. I was relatively new here.

"I'm Kat Devereaux, and you I presume are Viktor?

"You presume correctly. Welcome to my club. I hope you enjoy yourself."
He approached me like a cat, in silence and with no discernable movement. Suddenly he was just there with his arm around me looking down into my eyes.

I blinked and blurted out. "Can I talk to you in private?" Probably not my smartest move. Duh, ask the sexy vampire to take you somewhere private. What do think he's gonna think?

"My pleasure." Oh goody I thought as he led me through crowds that I couldn't part with a bulldozer and soon we were in his private office. He pounced on me instantly and plundered my open mouth before I could say a word. Damn if he couldn't kiss as good as his brother. My mind tried to surface to remember why I was there. I pushed away from him with one hand on his chest and the other holding his arm to keep from falling down as I struggled out of the embrace.

Leslie Brown   39

"Whoa there studly, you may have misunderstood my intentions."

He laughed and slouched sexily. "Darlin' I hope they're as lecherous as mine."

Oops, deep shit again. Oh well, I might as well dive deeper. "I'm not here to seduce you. I know you're a vampire and I want you to make me a vampire too."

He wasn't laughing any more. "What ever gave you that idea?"

I just blurted out my reason for being there. "Your brother Tarik told me you are a vampire and that he made you."

"My brother is dead. You couldn't possibly have talked to him." He grabbed my arms and all but screamed down my throat.

"You're right he is dead, but he's just not in his coffin anymore. I let him go. He's been out for several months now and knows you're here."

"If you let him out then make him turn you. It's his specialty!" He yelled at me and released me, giving me a shove towards the door.

I turned back and pleaded. "Please help me. I know this seems crazy but if you do this you will save my life and my sister's life."

"Why won't he do it? He certainly had no qualms about doing it to me."

"Tarik has sworn never to turn another human being again. He feels terrible for making you suffer."

"Maybe I should do it then. I owe him one and this should make us even."

My stomach fluttered. I was scared. This is not how I wanted this to happen, out of revenge. I turned as if to go when he grabbed my arm and spun me around.

"Not chickening out are you?" He licked my neck and nibbled my ear. His other hand held me up and one thumb rubbed my nipple through my t-shirt. Damn it I should have worn a bra!

"I'm not sure this is how I want this." He ravaged my mouth once again as the door burst open. Tarik stood there and looked at us with fury in his eyes.

Deja Voodoo

"So I see you decided to get it elsewhere. Why am I not surprised you had to choose my brother."

I disengaged myself from Viktor and faced Tarik with my own rage.

"What did you expect? You wouldn't do it! You two are the only vampires I know." I just glared at them both with my hands on my hips.

"If either of you comes to your senses I'm sure you can find me!" I slammed the door on my way out leaving them alone.

Chapter 12

    I felt so guilty when Tarik walked in on me with Viktor. The look he gave me when his brother was pawing and slobbering on me was horrible. The realization had hit me when I was in Viktor's office. I was more than a little in love with Tarik. It should be something to make me happy but I was miserable. I knew that he was never going to give in and I was never going to give up. Either way it would tear us apart but there was nothing I could do about it. It wasn't just me that I had to worry about. My sister needed me and I couldn't let her down.

    He came to me before dawn and I was waiting for him. He slipped into the bed with me, our naked bodies pressed together just holding each other. I cried in his arms, "I love you." He still would not give in. If it was just me I would give in to him and live for just the time we had but this was not just about me. My sister must have felt this way when she gave in. I knew how she felt now and thought about her as I slept. When I woke he was gone.

    I knew that I would see him again someday but it would never be the same. I called the club and left a message for Viktor that I wanted to see him. There was no time to spare my sister's baby was due very soon. I went through my daily activities at work and painted every day but I put the paintings of Tarik away. I couldn't bear to look at them.

    The second night after I had sent the message to Viktor he came to me just as his brother had through the window. I explained to him what I needed him for and how Tarik would not help me because of what he had done to him. Viktor told me that he was no longer angry about his state of being. He had come to terms with it years before and had been searching for his brother's lost coffin for years so that he could set Tarik free and make up with his brother.

    "Are you sure this is what you want?" He approached me slowly like he didn't want to spook me.

    "Yes, I'm certain. This is the only way left for me." I thought he would just come and do it but we spent several hours talking. Viktor told me what to expect and how it would feel, how to survive and what precautions to take. I would be as if dead for three days and then rise so we needed a safe place to hide me. I told him of a crypt in Odd Fellows Cemetery that was empty. We agreed to meet in the cemetery the next week to give me time to prepare and plan. I couldn't just disappear for three days. I had a business to run and people would notice if I was suddenly missing.

Viktor told me that there was a chain of hotels he owned that was safe to stay in during the day. The undead jokingly refer to it as Motel 666. I made reservations for the trip to my Sister's place in Wyoming. I told Skye I would be gone for a few weeks to help my sister. I had contractors working in my bedroom to create a "safe room" to sleep in during the day. Everything was set up and ready, all that was left was for me to die. I called Alex and told her my plan and she wished me luck but told me if I couldn't do it she understood. That just strengthened my resolve more. I sat by the river and wrote a note and poem to Tarik and left it on my bed.

When this is over I will explain why it had to be this way.

The last sunset looms before me
Reflected in muddy depths.
As a relic of times passage paddles by.
Shall I remember this haunted past
As the future fades in history?
The pain of losing those you love
Of secrets kept, tears wept.
Will I regret, strangle in this
Dark eternity I have chosen?
Or shall I embrace deaths
Lure of immortality?
For this is the path I have chosen
Forsaken soul bartered for love.
The toll freely paid in exchange
To end this repetitious curse.
For this endless Déjà vu

In which I'm trapped.
A life which posses but one key
Freedom lies with immortality.

Forgive me.
Kat

Chapter 13

I planned to meet Viktor at Odd Fellows Rest at midnight.
I took the streetcar on Canal to meet him there. The moon was
full and I had spent the sunset at the river soaking in the last rays
of the sun. I thought that is what I would miss most, the sunrise,

and sunset. The full moon lit the way through the cemetery to Daniel's grave. I had thought that Daniel might not mind rooming with me for a few days. We had just finished restoring his tomb and all of the ashes and bones had been cleared to the bottom of the crypt. The upper shelf was relatively clean for me to spend my three days dead. When we had begun restoration on Odd Fellows the gates had fallen down and homeless people were sleeping in the open crypts. If they could do it then so could I.

Many people don't realize that the tombs are used repeatedly. When a person is sealed inside the tomb it takes a year in the sultry heat to cremate the deceased naturally. One year and one day later the tomb is opened and the ashes moved to the bottom leaving room to bury someone else. If more than one family member dies in the year a temporary location can be use called the vaults or ovens. Those are the wall like tombs that have many small spaces for single burials of for people who can't afford or do not want a crypt.

I entered the cemetery with the key I used to help with restorations. Open gates left the cemetery prime for grave robbers. The saying goes that if you want to see the best New Orleans cemetery art you have to go to California. Many artifacts will never be returned due to theft. I hope that we can prevent more pillaging at these cemeteries with help from organizations like Save Our Cemeteries.

The night was chilly and I drew my hoodie over my head as I made my way towards the tomb. In the center of the cemetery I saw him waiting for me. I guess vampires have "skills" because the gate was locked yet here he was. His back was to me and he was wearing a dark hooded cloak. Vampires are way theatrical. As I approached he slowly turned and his hood fell away so that I could see his face.

"Tarik! What are you doing here? You can't stop me; I have made up my mind." I planted my boots stubbornly and crossed my arms and looked around for Viktor.

Tarik spoke softly, "I know I cannot stop you. Viktor came to me and told me of your plan. He made me realize that I had no choice in your decision. However, I do have a choice in how this will happen. If it has to happen it will be me, not him. I love you too much to let him be the one to do this."

I gasped in shock at both revelations. First he loved me and second he would do it. I was overjoyed and blurted, "You have no idea what this means to me. When this is over I will tell you everything and you will understand why I have been so secretive. We can start new and..."

He cut me off, "there will be no after. I may have to help kill you but I can't stay here and watch you become a monster like me. When you wake I won't be here. Viktor will help you acclimate yourself to being undead. I am leaving."

I felt like someone had kicked me in the gut. All the air had deflated from my lungs. He wouldn't be here? The numbness sunk in and I asked, "Where are you going?" I was hoping that he just had a business trip planned but knew that wasn't it.

"I can't watch this, I am leaving, I don't know where just away. He stood there stiff and straight looking like a marble statue. More beautiful than any piece of art. He reached the short distance between us and drew me into his arms.

He kissed me like he would devour me whole. This kiss was one which you know there is no return. Every kiss before I knew it was just that, a kiss. This time there was no turning back. Now I would gladly abandon myself to this point of no return. I had waited 26 years for this moment. My hands slid beneath his jacket and over his stone carved abdomen, up and over his shoulders. His jacket slid to the ground in a pool of ebony.

I could tell by the cold temperature of his body that he had not fed this evening. He had always been careful before to feed before seeing me. He was always warm after feeding but now his skin truly felt like marble. It registered in the back of my mind why he had not fed. I would be dinner tonight, chilling. The cold October night cooled me as well but on the inside I was boiling. This might be my only night with him and I intend to enjoy it. I reached for the tie holding back his long silken hair. Mine was so curly it was a sensual treat to run my fingers through his straight flowing strands. The full moon glittered on each black sliver revealing a myriad of colors from indigo to the deepest purple. Laying against his pale skin the contrast of dark and light was startling.

Tarik was built like a swimmer with so many definitions in the muscles on his chest and abdomen I felt my way through them like a blind person learning every nook and cranny. I was five feet 9, taller than all of my friends I had always felt freakish. Tarik was almost a foot taller than me and he made me feel tiny. I unbuttoned the remainder of his shirt and tugged it from his pants letting it join his jacket on the grassy mound in the center of the cemetery. At this point I had lost any semblance of shyness and completely undressed him without interruption. He stood before me in his full glory as God or possibly the Devil intended him to be. Hollywood hunks would pale in comparison to this man.

I stood back staring as I heard him chuckle and utter, have you looked your fill?" I felt the blood run to my cheeks as I realized I had been staring for quite some time. "I've never seen anyone so beautiful" I stammered. In college I had to draw nudes in art class. When the male models showed up it was like the coffee commercial with Juan Valdez where everyone goes to one side of the ship and it tips to that side. We all ran to the model's backside to avoid having to draw the obvious. I didn't have to try very hard not to see those models but I couldn't take my eyes off of Tarik.

He broke my hypnotic trancelike state by drawing my jacket off and tossing it on the growing pile of clothes. Soon I was just as naked as him but much more self conscious, and suddenly felt shy. As I stood there I watched the emotion play on his features as he took his time perusing me as I had ogled him. I guess one good turn deserved another. I wasn't sure if it was the cold air or his gaze that puckered my nipples but I think it was just him. His large hand gently cupped one peaking globe as he pulled me to him claiming my mouth again.

There must be a class for vampires to learn how to kiss because he excelled in that art. I could feel his sharp fangs with my tongue and as one nicked me he licked it to seal the wound. Viktor had told me that vampires could seal wounds with their saliva. I had learned a lot in the time that I had planned for my death including the fact that we could not consummate this act until Tarik had fed. A vampire needed blood to get an erection so for now he lay soft and supple in my hands as I took the

Leslie Brown   47

opportunity to explore. I had felt him while he was fully aroused and knew what was in store for me but this was an unexpected pleasure.

Tarik explored my curves as well with hands, tongue, and lips drawing incoherent mutterings and moaning from my own lips. His hands reminded me that this was a double edged sword. I could touch him endlessly but I knew that if I didn't push him we would get nowhere. I licked and bit my way up his chest to his neck where I clamped down and sucked as if I were the vampire and he the meal. He sucked in a breath and pulled me off of him. I could see that his green eyes had gone black. He was struggling to keep himself under control. I reached up and pulled my hair back revealing my pulsing neck. It was like dangling crack in front of an addict. He roared and lunged for me in one explosive move.

His fangs pierced my neck and the pain was instantly transformed into a knee buckling orgasm. Hey, I had been celibate, not stupid I knew how an orgasm felt. I felt like I was going to die, explode, or just spontaneously combust. In a few moments I began to feel dizzy like I had drunk one too many margaritas. He lowered me to the bed of discarded clothing in the center of a cemetery and plunged his straining erection into me. The virginal barrier finally breached in a stroke of ecstasy I had never imagined.

He glided in and out of me while still drinking from my neck. The feeling of him inside of me was so intoxicating. I had imagined this a thousand times but never came close to the feelings I now felt. It was like he was drawing something from deep inside me through the veins at which he fed. His rhythm slowed and brought a different type of exquisite torture. My spine bowed as I felt the end coming. Soon the orgasm built within me to match his inevitable one. We came together in an explosion of waves followed by the crashing shore of death. I looked into his eyes and saw tears as he bit into his own wrist and held it to my lips. I could see the sorrow I had caused this man I loved and owed my life to him. I had forced him to do that which he had sworn never to do again. That was the last thought to fill my mind as everything turned black and became nothing.

Deja Voodoo

A flash of lightning followed by thunder lit up the night and in her tomb the priestess stirred. It was the unraveling of the curse that woke her. "Soon we will be together my love."

Chapter 14

I woke in Daniel's tomb. My first thought was surprise that it actually worked. My second thought was what was that poking my butt. I reached under and pulled out a femur bone. "Oh, my bad. Sorry Daniel, I'll put it back."

"No shit you'll put it back!"

I jerked up and promptly hit my head on the ceiling.

"Who's there? I asked in the dark.

"Duh, it's me Daniel. You know the guy whose side of the grave you are hogging. Your three days are up so please remove your carcass from my bed!"

"Hey, we moved all of your bones to the bottom shelf" I argued.

"This is my tomb and I don't like the bottom. I like my stuff up here."

Just then I heard someone approach and the marble façade moved sideways. It was Viktor just as he had promised. No matter what he had said I still hoped that Tarik would be there. I ungracefully scooted out and was happy to see Tarik had dressed me before depositing me in the vault. Before returning the face to the tomb I gently scooted the bones back in place and apologized to Daniel.

"Sorry I displaced your bones. Is there anything I can do to make it up to you?"
I could see the ghostly body of Daniel now that it was lighter. In fact I could see everything much more clearly and there were many ghosts standing around staring at us. One of them spoke.

"Thanks for the show the other night. We don't get out much so it's nice to have entertainment brought in." I cringed thinking of the show that we must have put on for all the ghosts to see.

Another chimed in, "When are you going to fix my tomb?" Then a whole chorus of ghosts started making more requests. My name is misspelled, the date is wrong, that's not my tomb, etc. I could see and hear them all clearly now. Before I sometimes heard them but this was so cool. I promised to come back and make a list of their requests so that I could carry out their wishes later. I always knew they could tell if they had been taken care of. This new knowledge just made me more determined to take care of the cemeteries.

We left the cemetery behind and hopped on the streetcar. As we neared the French Quarter I couldn't help but notice that everything was much brighter, the colors more vivid. In the cemetery things were more muted, almost black and white like an old photograph but still brighter than before.

"Does everything look this vivid to you?" I asked Viktor.

"You will get used to it. It's like having cat vision. No pun intended."

We got off at Bourbon Street and walked toward the crowds. It was Saturday night every night on Bourbon Street and tonight was even worse with the pre-Halloween crowd. We entered one of the many strip clubs and Viktor led me to a back room where a young man sat alone. I assumed he was one of the strippers from his state of undress. He was kind of delicate and too pretty to be handsome. In this town it was even hard to tell what is female and what is male but he was definitely the later. He seemed to be permanently saluting someone if you know what I mean? Viktor told me he was a donor and was O.K. with me drinking from him. It creeped me out that he seemed so needy and such a perpetual victim. Even so, I was unable to deny the thirst. My fangs extended in anticipation and I took his word for it and latched on to the man's jugular faster than you can say 'happy meal". I thought it would be icky but it tasted more like honey, sticky and sweet, a little bit metallic, definitely yummy. I knew this was what I would have to do but the reality was quite surreal.

After a minute Viktor pulled me back and said, "Enough. That will do for now." I leaned in for one final wound sealing swipe of my tongue concentrating on healing his wound. Viktor had explained the way vampires healed was by sending a mental message to release the power. He slipped the donor several hundred dollar bills and we left. I wondered how often a person could donate blood and asked Viktor as we left the club. "Once or twice a week at most," he replied.

After a couple more donors and a few lessons on survival we walked up Dumaine to Royal and into my apartment. Viktor explained that at first I would need to feed often but the need would lessen. He let me in through the gallery with his own key. While I had been gone Viktor had been busy overseeing the work transforming my home to make it safe. The windows were now shuttered with black out tint on the glass. When I slept no one could get inside easily. There was also what I had described to Skye as a panic room for me to sleep in. It had a day bed inside and a fridge filled with bottled blood, comfy enough for the dead.

Leslie Brown

Later when I entered the gallery I sensed a presence. Warily I ascended the staircase following my senses. A ghost was perched on the edge of my antique bed looking quite miffed. Her arms were crossed and her toe was tapping in aggravation. I had an idea who it was by the fact that she was completely naked.

"Julie?" I asked the apparition. The building had been owned by a beautiful Octoroon mistress who had tragically frozen to death on the roof waiting for her lover to marry her. Julie was 1/8 African American and lived here in the 1800's.

"Who else would it be here in my own house girl?"

I tried to start over "I'm sorry, I was just startled to see you. Apparently my seeing ghosts, was not going to be limited to cemeteries. What can I do for you?" I asked her as she rose and paced the floor.

"Nothin' just now. I just wanted to see what was happening around here. I seen all the men workin' and just was curious." With that she just faded away.

For the next two nights Viktor showed me how to hunt and cloud the minds of my prey. As I had surmised you can find plenty of food on the child predator web sites. I ran into many more of the ghosts and was learning to deal with them. Most just acted like the living people going about their nightly activities but some wanted to interact. I was learning to find donors and living my new existence. In the beginning I chose those willing to donate for money. I learned to recognize my own kind and be wary of them. One night shortly after rising I went out to find dinner. I wasn't looking for a donor just yet, I had snacked from the fridge. What I needed was a juicy steak. I could still eat but only felt the need infrequently. The place I was headed to had the best steaks and seafood in town. It wasn't one of those highly publicized places though. The shack of a restaurant was on the river and I had to drive there in my Jeep

I drove out of the parking garage that was near the gallery and headed toward Algiers over the river. The place was downriver from New Orleans and catered mainly to locals. The parking lot was still full at eleven thirty. Even away from the city night life was busy on a Saturday. I chose a seat at the bar and ordered a steak, rare along with an ice cold pint of Abita beer.

The steak was superb and I finished and left a generous tip heading out to the Jeep. As I dug in my backpack for the keys I realized I wasn't alone.

There were two other vampires in the parking lot and they were flanking me. This did not look good. They slowly approached me. "Lookey what we got here. Smells like fresh meat." The vampire to my right said. He looked menacing in a psyco vampire kind of biker type. His friend didn't look much better. Viktor had warned me about just this type of situation. His words echoed in my brain. "Don't get trapped outside of my territory, I might not be able to save you pretty ass." At the time he just annoyed me but it looked like he was right.

"What-chu doin' on my side o' the river sugar?" He moved closer, mimicked by his friend who said; "Maybe she needs to pay the toll." This was not looking good. "Sorry guys, I just came here for the steak. Just helping out the local economy via tourism." I tried to smile but nervously showed a little too much fang. They were on me in a half a heartbeat.

Before I could think of a way out of this I heard Viktor's voice. "Leave her alone." They didn't let me go but the one who had grabbed my boob let go and his friend removed his tongue from my ear. Ew! Thank God for the cavalry. One attacker turned away and spoke to Viktor. "This is our territory Vik, she crossed the river. That makes this her dinner or least a ways the appetizer." "Not this one, she's off limits. This is Tarik's girl. You touch her you answer to him."

He looked surprised. "No shit? Tarik's back?" "Yes, he's back and he would fry your ass for harming one hair on her head. The two goons let go of me and backed away from Viktor. "Sorry, no harm chere' we din' know who you was." They turned and quickly disappeared.

Viktor grabbed my elbow and half drug me around the side of the Jeep to the passenger side. He opened the door and I got in without question knowing I had screwed up. Halfway back to New Orleans he started in on me.

"I told you to stay close to home. How do I keep an eye on you and keep you safe if you wander into enemy territory. Lucky for you we have a pact with the vampires on that side of the river."

"Sorry, I wasn't thinking. I just wanted to get out and I had a fierce craving for a steak." We drove the rest of the way home and he parked the Jeep in my assigned spot in the garage. "How did you find me?" We got out and Viktor came around to my side. He leaned over me placing his hands on either side of the roll bars. "I'd hate for you to make a rookie mistake and get gobbled up. I want to save that pleasure for myself."

I ducked down under his arms and heard him laugh as I returned to the safety of my home. Point taken, I would definitely be more careful from now on. I didn't know much about the territory thing and I wasn't going to take any more chances.

Chapter 15

One week after I rose as a vampire I packed my Jeep and headed west to save my sister. I planned to end the death curse that had haunted my family for over a hundred years. My itinerary had been posted with the territory alliance and I was free to travel unmolested. Viktor had given me an identification card to show when I checked into "Motel 666". This was a private membership for owners and partners in the corporation that owned the chain. In my room the windows were tinted and heavy curtains could black out the sun. The bed rose up on hydraulics to reveal a small space underneath in which to sleep. The do not disturb signs were quite amusing. There were several to choose from but Viktor told me to use the one that said, "Dead to the world, do not disturb".

The trip to Wyoming shouldn't take more than three nights if I hauled ass that is. I spent two days holed up just to be careful and not get caught out. I had an emergency bag in my Jeep as well that could do in a pinch. It was sort of like those survival blankets that look like aluminum foil only this was like a jiffy pop cadaver bag. If I had to I could get off the road and to hide in it. That would do as long as no one found me and got curious. A few vamps had been found in their port-a-coffins and been fried instantly. The humans that found them had been deemed crazy by the authorities but the word had spread via the internet and vamps were more careful now where they hid.

As I drove to my sister's home I thought about all the new things I was dealing with. I had known what to expect but the reality was still shocking. My tan was fading but thanks to spray on tans I was compensating and covering my new paleness. The best side effect was no more bad hair days. I always woke up with perfect hair which I really loved. All my life I had fought the frizzies and tangles. No more though now my hair was perfectly manageable.

I arrived in the middle of the night and found Alex asleep next to Luke. I didn't want to scare them but that's exactly what I did. He woke up first and screamed like a girl. I had to suppress a laugh, not wanting to make a really bad impression. Alex woke and looked relieved to see me. She rolled to her side and sat up revealing her rounded belly. I crumbled to the floor and wrapped my arms around her crying in relief. I had made it in time. She shushed me and stroked my head while holding me tight.

We only had each other since Dad had passed away and this was the longest amount of time we had ever been apart. I crawled up to the bed and sat next to Alex and she introduced me to Luke.

Leslie Brown

"Kat, this is Luke." She looked so hopeful and I'm sure she worried that I would not think him worthy considering she thought he was worth dying for. Who was I to judge I had just done that very same thing. We talked for a while I decided she had done the right thing. They were made for each other.

"Luke, honey could you please go brew us some of your delicious hot chocolate?" Sam's request was code for: leave us alone so we can talk. As he left the room I had to notice he was awfully cute in his Scooby Doo boxers. Alex and I had opposite tastes though. I like tall dark and fangsome and she went for the blonde adrenaline jockey. Luke is a professional snowboarder and they had met on the mountains in Colorado.

After he shut the door I could hear his footsteps and puttering in the kitchen I asked her, "how many seconds did you hold out after you met him?" Alex slapped me with a pillow and we both started giggling like when we were kids. It was so good to see her. When you are so busy you don't think about little things like sitting and giggling over a cute guy. "I've missed you so much," I told Alex. She said, "ditto kiddo," that was a thing we always said to each other.

"O.K. so show me your fangs countess" she asked and gave me that look.

"It was the only way," I said and then I smiled showing off my sharp new choppers as I let them slide out of hiding. "Holy shit! You're- it's real. You really did it?"

I retracted my fangs tactfully like a cat putting away its claws. "Of course I really did it. I would do anything for you, for us. Our family has suffered long enough."

She could see the shadow coming towards her. The Baron held her in his tight embrace. "Not yet, his soul is not joined yet but de time be near."

She reached for me and hugged me and whispered, "Just keep your fangs off of Luke. I'm the only one who gets to suck anything on him," we both rolled over laughing hysterically. I laid my ear on her belly and listened to the baby. "I can hear her heartbeat." Alex smiled and said, "She's coming soon. We need to make plans." We talked and Alex told me that she planned to have the birth at home. Alex had told Luke that I was a midwife

Deja Voodoo

and I would be there to help. She also told him he could not be there, claiming that she didn't want him to see the icky parts. Alex had a friend who was an Indian healer who would help us.

Luke joined us with a tray filled with three steaming mugs. I pretended to drink mine and surreptitiously slipped it to Alex when he wasn't looking. I was not a fan of hot chocolate. I left them a little before dawn to get to "motel 666" in time to die. I claimed that I didn't want to be in the way, their only spare room was already transformed into a nursery. Every evening I spent with Alex teaching her about her new life.

Several nights after I had arrived I woke early. It was time and the baby was coming. I could feel Alex's pain and I knew I had to get to her fast. I waited impatiently sensing when the sun had finally set and rushed to her. The healer was already there and Luke gave me a funny look that said, "where have you been?" Alex was between contractions and said, "I told you she would get here in time." She smiled at Luke and told him "now just go out and pace the living room floor". He leaned over her and asked, "are you sure?" "Yes, no kiss me and go!" He did as she ordered and gave me one last look and mouthed, "take care of them".

Just then another contraction took hold of her and Alex screamed. They were coming closer and closer. I looked at Alex and said, "I have to tell her now" motioning at Billie, the healer. Alex nodded and squeezed my hand as I explained between contractions what I was and what was going to happen. The plan was to let Alex have the baby and then I would quickly take her blood and give her mine. The hardest part would be explaining to Luke why Alex was dead. Surely he couldn't bitch much it would only be for three days as opposed to forever. With one last painful contraction the baby came out, I bit into Alex's neck.

The vision became clear as she watched the spirit join with her lover, body and soul together. They held each asked; "Papa Legba end the curse, set us all free."

Chapter 16

I hate it when I'm right. It was extremely hard to get Luke
to understand that she was not dead for real. I had to extend my
fangs and get in his face to get my point across. Billie confirmed
what I told him and the new baby finally gave him something to
focus on. Alex had written a letter that I gave him before leaving.
I carried Alex to my car and then drove to the motel where she
would be safe in the second hide-a-crypt in my hotel room.

Deja Voodoo

Three days later Alex rose and I showed her the ropes so to speak, after feeding for the first time Alex returned to her home to meet her baby. It was a bittersweet scene for me as I would never know the joy of having my own child. Vampires rarely conceived and if they did the baby almost never survived.

I stayed with them for a month and reluctantly left to return to my own life. The drive back was so much less stressful it seemed like it took half the time. There were several customers needing consults on commissions and my inventory had dwindled away. I got busy painting every night to make up for the lost time. Mardi Gras was just a few weeks away and I needed to have a surplus of art ready. My routine was to wake, hunt, feed, paint, and then play.

It was so interesting hanging out at the cemeteries and listening to the ghosts requests. I wrote everything down and began archiving info to keep records. Daniel was a great help and proved invaluable. He was adept at fending off overzealous requests and kept the droves at bay so I could tackle one request at a time. I kept the restorers busy with my many requests and they were planning a gala fundraiser. Julie was always at my side as I recorded all of the information in the computer that the other ghosts had given me. When she saw one entry she insisted, "don't you believe that Sarah James. She always lied about her age." It was so funny the way they acted just like live people squabbling, gossiping, and whining. Julie was a pampered and educated woman but still loved to gossip.

Some nights I would go to Club Morte and see Viktor. It was on my most recent visit that several things happened. Viktor had repeatedly told me that if Tarik did not want to be found I would not find him. I started bugging him again and he led me back to his office and slammed the door.

"I told you that when he made me Tarik hid for over 100 years. If he wants to stay hidden you won't find him period!" Viktor had been coming on quite strong lately and I was sure he was trying to force me into a more intimate relationship with him. Viktor proved my theory when he pulled me into his arms and gently kissed me. It took me by surprise with his gentle onslaught. I might have expected a full on assault but not this. Viktor was the tattooed, pierced bad boy, not the sensitive lover.

He lightly held my face in his hands and tentatively kissed me. His lips were full and decadently sensual and as I had learned before he was a master at the art of kissing. I didn't know such a gentle kiss could hold so much power. I reluctantly pulled away from him and tried to regain my composure. That kiss wasn't just Viktor teasing and flirting, trying to get into my coffin. There were some deep feelings exposed it seemed. This was so totally unexpected I didn't know how to react. He broke my analytical reverie and gave me his roguish grin while taunting me.

"Just think what else these lips can do Kitty Kat." He purred and grinned at me making my stomach turn flip flops. He was a piece of Goth candy dripping in chocolate leather. Viktor wore his usual floor length coat and matching pants were painted on in a glorious shade of rust to match his hair and golden eyes. His nipples were adorned with golden loops to match his ears and eyebrow rings. The tattoos spread down his bare chest and disappeared into his pants. A girl could spend hours licking her way over them and...

"Hungry?" Viktor asked. Damn if I didn't just lick my lips! I shook myself out of it and pushed him away and out of my lurid thoughts.

"You wish!" He laughed and it was like honey dripping over my skin. Damn he was sexy. Viktor walked to his desk and I was sure he was posing. He leaned halfway on and halfway off the desk and caressed a laptop saying, "I got you a present".
That curiosity got me again and I stalked over in my own sexy black leather outfit. I couldn't help but look at the line of muscle that ran from the edge of his abs down and into his pants. God I am a sucker for washboard abs. He grinned and managed to thrust himself at me as he rolled off the desk and presented the laptop to me. Immediately my suspicions were up. This was no ordinary laptop. The computer was a top of the line custom made Alienware, a $7000 laptop. I knew this because I have been secretly coveting the Alien models for a while now. I put two and two together and naturally the answer was sex. He was trying to buy me.

"Just what the hell am I supposed to give you for this?" I crossed my arms and tapped my foot in anger.

Dawning poured over his face and he blurted, "it's not from me. It is a part of a job offer from the vampire council. Do you remember when you kidded me about your becoming a vampire?" I looked a question mark at him and he continued. "You said that you would have to watch out for holy water loaded squirt guns and tanning beds." I nodded vaguely remembering a conversation we had months ago.

"That gave me some ideas and I have been acting on them in preparation for this day. You are new and have a fresh eye. You see things that those of us who measure our lives in centuries cannot. We need your help." He walked around the desk and sat, gesturing for me to do the same. I did so and waited to hear more. Obviously the seduction portion of the program was over and it was time for business.

"There is a group of vampires that oversee the welfare of humans and our kind. I am part of that group. There is a delicate balance between the races. To keep the balance sometimes we have to cull the herd so to speak. That's where you can help. Your tanning bed notion gave me the idea. You are a perfect candidate to be an assassin for the council."

He waited for all that to sink in and watched my reaction. I must have looked like a fish with my mouth opening and closing in succession. Thoughts raced through my mind. Slowly I formed my thoughts into questions which he answered patiently.

"Assasin? Just what do you do in this organization?" He replied, "I am the leader for the city of New Orleans. Some lead entire states but Louisiana is divided since we have such a large vampire population, the highest in the United States actually."

"What do you do as the leader?" He shifted in his chair and answered patiently. "As the leader I have to keep order within the vampire and other non-human and non-living inhabitant's lives. I keep the peace and keep the secrets. Cover up awkward situations, mediate between species, and determine who must be terminated. The biggest rule is to keep invisible. Humans must not know we are real. We depend on them for sustenance; therefore we must keep them safe."

"And I thought you were just another pretty face. This is all very interesting but I have a job and I don't think I want to help kill anyone, even If they are already dead."

Leslie Brown

"I thought you might say that. Do you think that I haven't noticed that you have been feeding strictly off of the child predator database?" He stood up and paced like a caged lion, slowly stalking back and forth. "There are worse things than your run of the mill sex offender." I couldn't imagine worse than some that I had seen. My vampire abilities allow me to see into the minds of the men I have fed from. I try not to destroy them but clouding their minds makes me feel better. Generally I implant the thought that kids make the molesters violently sick. When they are in the presence of any kids they get so sick they avoid kids forever. It works for me. It's my own little form of vigilante justice.

"We have our own version of the most abhorred, for instance this fine gentleman." Viktor dropped a file in my lap and proceeded speaking. "Meet your first assignment. He's a very handsome and likeable guy, but he is the worst type of monster imaginable. A child molester is just an animal but this man is a true beast. He kidnaps children as young as a year old and turns them into vampires to work in his psychopathic whorehouse. He keeps them for the sickest sort of molester to pay for what they want. These children only last a few months to a few years before becoming completely insane and turn revenant. They become mindless feeders who attack and kill anyone in sight and have to be destroyed."

I felt sick to my stomach. The folder was filled with photographs of unspeakable things. I snapped it closed and said, "I'm in."

Viktor smiled and sat in his big leather chair. He turned the laptop towards me and the screen showed a page asking for a name and password. "Please create a name and password. This will get you into the VampNet site. I did so and the screen welcomed me. The greeting stated that I would be paid commissions per each piece of art completed. Funds would be routed directly to my account at completion. Each job would pay according to degree of difficulty. Any time I wanted I could access the site and select a target. The inference was that I would be painting portraits.

I clicked on the first file to open it. Inside was a photo of the man in the folder I held. The commission price for him was $200,000. "Is this correct?"

"Oh, it's quite correct. You are a very highly sought after artist, worth every penny to do this work."

For an asshole like this I would kill him free and call it community service. But getting paid just sounded like gravy. "I accept," I said.

"Perfect, now let's just go over my plans. Viktor told me how he planned for me to do the job. We left the club and headed to the Garden District where he lived. I had been to his home once before and this house was not far away and still just as lavish. The home was on Prytania Street and was of course historical for some reason I couldn't quite recall from a walking tour I had taken when I first moved to New Orleans over a year ago. We entered the house and proceeded directly up the grand staircase. Down the hall and to the right we entered the master bedroom suite. It was very pretty and feminine. There was a long wall with windows bordered by sheer drapes and a door I presumed led to a closet or restroom.

"After you.." Victor held the door and I went inside. It looked like a very ornate bathroom. I turned and Viktor flipped the light switch on. The door slammed shut with lightning speed and I could hear the main entry to the bedroom follow suit. I looked in the mirror realizing it was a two way mirror. The bedroom lit up brilliantly as a wall slid away and the windows revealed bright lights. "Ah, the tanning bed I presume?"

"Correct my dear. I stole the idea straight from your devious mind. We're going to give them a dose of good ole sunshine."

"Very devious indeed, I suppose that I am to lure the unsuspecting vampire to his own demise?" "Correct again, follow me."

We turned off the switch and waited for the room to be safe to enter. Then we went back through the bedroom and turned the opposite direction down the hall. There was a second master suite but it had a very different décor. Early Marquis de Sade I'd say. Obviously it was meant to entice the sicker side of my intended targets. It was set up exactly like the other and we

Leslie Brown   63

tried a few practice runs with the tanning lamps disengaged. It wouldn't do to let some vamp beat me through the door and find out what I had planned for him. Viktor turned the keys over to me and left me there to contemplate my future as an assassin.

Chapter 17

I was jumpy all week. Skye commented on it as I worked in my office on the new laptop. I nearly fell out of my chair when she came in the last time. Even Julie the ghost got me earlier in the week when she suddenly materialized and started bugging me about talking to her boyfriend. You would think that a little thing like death would make a girl give up on any thoughts of marriage but not Julie. Stubborn was her middle name. After all she did sit on her roof naked during a freezing storm to try and force him to marry her. I don't think that worked out very well.

After a week of stalking my prey I was ready to do this. My target was a regular freak but liked his women delicate and frilly. That meant the "D" word. I would have to wear a dress. It took me three hours to find one I could tolerate. I finally settled on a delicate number in a shade of light green to match my eyes. It was just sexy enough to garner interest and covered enough to keep me happy. I refused to budge on heels though and kept to a pair of ballerina style flats. Thanks to the miracles of being a vampire my hair was perfect and makeup unnecessary. I always wake up with perfect hair and my skin is flawless now. My perfectly manageable auburn curls flowed down my backless dress. I grabbed the purse I had bought to match the outfit because I had no pockets. A girl needs a place for keys, lipstick, and loaded squirt gun. I left the gallery and headed out into the night. My recognizance had helped determine a great place to pick up my target.

For a freak he sure had good taste. This party was a very private and difficult to get an invite if you were not 10 generations Creole. Many parties like this were popping up to welcome the Mardi Gras season. Viktor was on the Krewe and had secured me a coveted invitation to enter. I settled in a corner spot at the bar and deftly dodged hopeful pursuit. Before long my target took the bait and tried his hand at sweeping me off my feet.

"Hello gorgeous how is a pretty thing like you end up all alone?" God he was insufferable. The sad thing was that if I didn't know all that I did I might be not so nauseated by his drivel. He was handsome as the devil. I smiled and giggled and acted tipsy. We danced and I let him hold me a little too tight. Soon I asked him if he could see me home as I was afraid to drive. Naturally he agreed and the valet pulled up in a smarmy Corvette guaranteed to melt all the girls' panties.

I gave him directions between hiccups as his hand slid up my leg. When he pulled into the drive he lunged for me and assaulted my mouth with his fetid breath. I pulled back and uttered, "Slow down cowboy. I'm looking for a little more than 8 seconds." I opened the door and quickly ran up the walk with him hot on my tail. Fumbling in the unaccustomed purse I found the keys and opened the door. We entered and as I shut the door he pinned me to the door. One hand grabbed my ass and the other dove into my cleavage. I didn't think I just reacted. I slapped at him and shoved him away.

"I can see you need to be taught some manners!" I stood with my hands on my hips and tried to think. It worked and he looked quite contrite so I went with it. "Go upstairs!" I ordered him to my room, the naughty one. "Take off your clothes and get on the bed!" I yelled at him. "And don't move!" I pointed to the naughty bedroom. I walked through the bathroom door as he complied. One quick flick of the switch and he was toast. It was just so easy. I flipped off the switch and waited until it was safe to enter. That worked quite well. I retrieved the keys from his discarded pants and dumped the Vette in the city. It was much easier than I had ever thought it would be. A cleaning crew took care of the mess and I was $200,000 richer not to mention one more freak of the streets. I donated half to the cemetery restoration funds and the other to a shelter for abused women and children and hoped it would help my conscience. It's hard to feel bad though when the bastard deserves it. Besides he was already dead, I just persuaded him to lie down permanently.

Chapter 18

Almost a year had gone by since I died and returned as a vampire. I had still not seen Tarik since that night but his brother Viktor was nearly impossible to avoid. Tarik filled my dreams with the memory of our one night together as lovers. Viktor filled my nights with sweet torture and the possibility of fulfillment. Deep within my soul Tarik is always there, a part of me, everything I could ever want, yet out of grasp. Viktor on the other hand is very much within my grasp. Every time we meet and go over my assignments it gets harder to resist the attraction.

Each night I wake and send mental images to Tarik of our night together, of my love for him but I do not know if they find him. I know the possibility exists because he did the same to me while he was trapped in his coffin. I imagine that my will to send thoughts to him must make it possible. Sometimes I just feel like a geek trying to do this. What if the messages get lost, end up at the wrong vampire. How embarrassing that would be. I have also received what I have termed teleporn- telepathic porn from Viktor. At times it is enough to send me over the edge.

His timing is uncanny, I'll be in the shower enjoying the solitude, and then he bursts in with visions of us together in the shower. The worst thing is that it feels so real but it leaves me feeling so empty and alone. It was just after a particularly lustful assault on my senses that I made a decision. I couldn't wait forever for Tarik. Forever was a very long time for an immortal. I had painted him a hundred times and cried a million tears but he might never return and I had to live with that. It was time to move on.

Mardi Gras was upon us again and I had asked Viktor to escort me to the Mourning Glory Ball for the cemeteries. We planned to show up in style in an antique hearse pulled by six black horses all decked out. I decided that after the ball I would talk to Viktor and set up an arrangement with him. I wasn't fooling myself, I knew I did not love him and vice versa. However, we did share a mutual case of extreme lust and it was time I fell off the wagon. I had waited 26 years and then only had one night and in a cemetery at that. It just wasn't fair. Tarik may choose to be alone but I didn't have to. And who knows if he is alone anyway. He is probably shacked up with some vamp tramp. Just the thought boiled my blood and strengthened my resolve. Victor and I could use each other for sex without any messy emotions involved.

The night of the ball I took extreme care getting ready. My costume was a complicated Victorian mourning gown of watered silk with a plunging neckline and a daring slit up one side all the way to my hips. Underneath was a torturous contraption in red and black guaranteed to drive Viktor crazy. The bustier ensured that my ample cleavage burst forth begging for attention and my long legs were clad in thigh high spider web hose attached with a garter. The matching thong almost covered and inch or two. I wore delicate lace up boots and my hair was piled high with tendrils escaping down my back. Topping it all off I wore a veiled hat and carried a riding crop. I'd smack anyone who interfered with my mission tonight.

I dressed at Viktor's Garden District home so that the hearse could meet us there. As I descended the stairs Viktor stood there looking splendid in his own Victorian waistcoat and breeches. The black just brought out the colors in his hair from blonde to copper to auburn. He still looked like the bad boy with all his piercings and tattoos. His shirt was opened and the sun tattoo around one nipple peeked out, others led the eye down, disappearing under cloth. He looked good enough to entice a nun to sin. He reminded me of a line in a song that says, "If I have to sin to see her again, then I'm gonna lie, lie, lie." That's how he makes me feel. It's wicked but worth damnation to indulge myself in his arms.

I greeted him with a deep kiss full of promise; my eyes told him of my decision. Surprise showed full upon his face and a little hint of panic. I said, "Don't worry; I won't respect you in the morning. I just plan to abuse you."

We left the house and proceeded to the hearse which was waiting. The interior was made to sit in rather than hold a coffin. The seats were of rich black leather. Curtains of velvet covered the windows. As soon as the door closed we came together in a frantic need mirrored in each other's eyes, we couldn't wait. These months had been tedious for us both. I had held back for so long.

His hands drove my dress up and my hands parted his shirt and delved for the opening in his pants. I freed him and was thankful he had fed already. One quick tug and my wisp of underwear were ripped away. Without a word he plunged into me and we found a jarring rhythm to match the beat of the carriage speeding through the streets. Our need exceeded any preliminaries as we mutually slammed into one another in a frenzy. When it was over I felt such a huge weight lifted from my

Deja Voodoo   68

shoulders. This was totally doable, I could manage to get laid and I didn't even feel guilty. It was exhilarating, liberating. Maybe it wasn't the best location but I felt like I had finally made a decision. I was completely in charge of my life and I was happy.

Chapter 19

We scrambled to restore order to our clothing, I put my boobs back in my dress and he managed to tuck himself away. By the time we had arrived at the masquerade ball we were respectably covered and grinning from ear to ear. We made the entrance of the evening in our hearse and a big crowd had turned out to see our arrival. We entered and the party was in full swing. The Kidney Thieves were on stage and there was a full house.

Viktor and I wound our way through the crowd and greeted each friend and acquaintance personally. We stayed within eyesight of each other and danced erotically to a slow song. The knowledge of what was to come later that night clearly preoccupying both our minds. I had to stay through the auction featuring my paintings and Skye's sculptures. She was there and in perfect form with her elaborate hair and costume. Skye towered over me in 8 inch heels and looked so exotic, like one of her sculptures come to life. She was a vamphaerie in black and purple.

The auction exceeded all our expectation and the members of the preservation group thanked everyone who donated and bought art. Thirty seconds later Viktor drug me by the hand out a side door where his black SUV waited. We didn't utter a word all the way to his house and I didn't argue about his choice of destination.

He left the car in the drive and we barely got in the door when Viktor backed me up against it. The urgency of before was still there but tempered with the knowledge that we were really doing this. Slowly and thoroughly he kissed me into ecstasy, probing every corner of my being with his deft tongue. Eventually his lips strayed allowing me my own exploration. He was so scrumptious I just wanted to bite him. I settled for restrained nibbles and licked my way around his pulsing neck. Each of us had fed earlier and therefore our hearts were actually beating. When vampires first rise in the evening they have no pulse. Right now mine was doing double time. I tugged at his pierced chin playfully with my teeth while craving the feel of flesh between them.

Viktor had the shoulders of my gown pulled down and the barest edge of my nipples threatened to spill out. Just then we heard a loud throat clearing and jumped away from each other in alarm.

"Tarik!" The last few hours replayed themselves through my mind in fast forward. I drank in his appearance as my mind raced. He was every bit as exotic and mouthwatering as I had remembered. He wore a tuxedo and in his hands a mask dangled. Dawning hit me all at once. He must have been at the ball. He most assuredly had seen us dancing and flirting. And with the spectacle we made just now I was completely mortified. Why hadn't I just waited? I was the epitome of patience and had waited 26 years for him the first time. Now look at me in one year I was giving up and giving in. He must think I am such a slut, and with his brother no less. Viktor and I were both speechless.

Tarik broke the silence with a snide comment. "What a pretty pair you two make. I hope you will be happy together." I ran to him and stopped just short of flinging myself in his arms. "It's not like that. We're not a pair, we're not anything." He sneered and said, "I can smell you on him, don't lie. It's not like I expected anything better from you!" He walked towards the door and paused as I confronted him with all the pent up frustration of the last year. "How would you know what I'm like you didn't stick around to find out you just ran away and hid. For your information I have only made love twice in my life. The first time was with you and the second was tonight after it was clear you had no interest in me and would never return. You didn't even stick around to see if I made it alright and to find out why I made you do this. You gave up the right to be pissed at me so don't even go there!" "You seem to have landed on your feet. I knew you were alright. How could I not know with all the mental images you keep sending me?" I thought maybe we would have a chance but I guess I was wrong. You don't need me." With that he turned and stalked out of the house.

After he left and I said an awkward goodnight to Viktor and I headed to my own home on Royal Street. Julie was in my room and badgered me about the evening. Apparently she was oblivious to my dark mood and felt free to annoy me. She doesn't leave the house except to go on the roof on the coldest of nights. Her lover never comes in the house he just appears on the balcony drinking the absinthe that killed him. Even in death they were both too stubborn to get their shit together. Since she didn't have a life literally and figuratively Julie lived vicariously through my experiences.

I told Julie about the costumes and the people at the ball "there were so many gorgeous gowns and masks. One lady had a mask that was so big I don't know how she held it up. The mourning costumes ranged from modern to mid 1800's styles."

Leslie Brown 71

"Were there many handsome gentlemen?" she asked expectantly. I went into detail describing several people who had made an impression on me. When Julie was finally satisfied she left me with a wistful sigh. I went to bed just as dawn arrived grateful that the sleep would stop my spinning thoughts.

All the next week I was grumpy and restless. I didn't know whether Tarik was still around or if he had skipped out again. I was furiously avoiding contact with Viktor and Skye was getting tired of making up excuses for me not returning his calls. I was out on a hunt for my newest target when Tarik finally appeared. The way he just popped up startled me and I squealed like a girl. I hate it when that happens. It doesn't do much for my big bad vampire slayer persona either. "Stop scaring me like that I squeeked at him." He just snickered and stood before me looking like a gallon of Hagen Daas and boy did I have a sweet fang. "I'm so sorry to have unduly startled you" he said rather facetiously "I thought it was time we talked." Without taking a breath he grilled me. ".Just what the hell are you doing with my brother? I can understand you have needs but that is just the kind of low blow I expect from a vampire!" His words angered me so bad I just wanted to hit him, the insufferable ass. "It's none of your business what I am doing. You walked out of my life and now you just pop back in and expect me to answer to you? I would have told you everything if you had just stuck around to listen. But no! You just ran away and hid and now you pop back into my life just when I've decided to get on with it. You think you have a say in what I do or who I see, you're crazy."" He looked completely nonplussed at my tirade and when I finished with a few other choice comments on his desertion he finally spoke. "Actually it is my business what you are up to. I'm your boss." I was floored, he must be joking. He was completely insufferable. "What the hell do you mean you're my boss?" I was really pissed now, nobody bosses me around. "Just because you took my virginity and turned me into a vampire does not mean you're the boss of me!" My cheeks reddened and anger flared in my eyes. He was really getting on my nerves. "I am the boss of you. Not because of the intimacy we shared but because I am the head of the vampire council for North America."

I couldn't have been more shocked. That meant that he was the boss of me and Viktor and every other vampire in America. Holy shit I had really stepped in it this time. I was beginning to wish I had left him in his coffin. I let this new information sink in and roll around in my head for a while. Finally showing some sense he actually let me think for a minute. "If you're my boss then you know what I am doing. I am on an assignment to rid the undead world of its rogue vampires. I'm using my skills for good, not evil.   Just because you're a vampire doesn't mean you have to be a socially irresponsible introverted hermit!"

He looked at me and said, "I am not talking about your assignment actually. I was referring to your relationship with my brother." That was just perfect. He was not only going to try and boss me around on assignments but in my personal life as well, ha! "My personal life is none of your concern." I said that and walked away. Well, honestly more like stomped away. How dare he come back and try to push me around. He had given up any hold he had on me, wrong again on that thought.

Chapter 20

I refused to let Tarik ruin my night. He may have come back but it was clear that he planned to control me. I've lived too long on my own without any man trying to do that, Tarik had better think again. If he had stayed with me instead of abandoning me things would have been way different.

I went to Viktor's home and waited for him to arrive. The night was beautiful and I went to the back patio to sit by the

Leslie Brown

glistening pool. Viktor arrived to find me sulking in a lounge chair. I stood and walked over facing him squarely in the chin. "I started this out with a decision to be with you and nothing has changed, I still want you. I reached one hand to the back of his neck to draw him closer for a kiss. He drew me in and looked me in the eye. "I don't want you here out of spite. I want you to want me." "I do want you."

Viktor tugged the t-shirt from my jeans and pulled it over my head. He carelessly tossed it to the ground and bent to savor one taught nipple after the other. Slowly my fingers crept through the knot of his tie until it too fell to the floor. I could feel the piercings in his nipples brushing against me through the fine silk of his shirt. My fangs extended like a lazy cats stretching and I knelt to bite away the buttons. One by one they popped off exposing the kaleidoscope of his flesh. Instead of his usual attire he was a wearing business suit for the meeting with the council which apparently was Tarik's real reason for being here.

Viktor shucked the remnants of the expensive shirt and I traced his tattoos with my fingertips. The pain he must have endured for each and every tattoo was unimaginable. Vampires heal so the only way to get tattoos is a very critical mixture of ink and holy water. The pain is a hundred times worse than human tattoos and a bad artist can screw up the mixture and scar you for eternity. I hate to think of the experimenting that it took to figure out the right mixture to complete the tattoo.

My fingers traced the radiant sun that encircled one pierced nipple. It puckered and shivered beneath my slight touch. I bent to taste the tender skin and tugged lightly at the silver ring drawing a gasp from Viktor. He shivered as I abandoned that task and began to lick and nip my way across his muscular chest and down to his belly button. I bit into the skin around it and sipped a few drops, licking the wound shut as I continued downward.

My hands trembled as I struggled to remove the belt that barred my way. Viktor's hands were tangled within my hair alternating between urging me on and holding me back. Right now I could tell he wasn't about to let me stop. I could feel how hard he was and nibbled at him through the cloth which only tortured him more. When Finally I began to release him the

Deja Voodoo

zipper was stuck from the pressure. He released my hair and himself in one fell swoop. As he sprang free I wrapped my lips around him and began to slide my way down as far as possible. Both hands encircled the shaft and I felt the pulse throbbing within. He held me away, drawing me to my feet and undid my jeans to slide them off.

He turned me around and held my breasts as he kissed my neck. Both nipples puckered as he teased them while piercing my skin to drink. I could swear the blood he drew came directly from deep down inside though he only took a sip before closing the wound. My knees buckled and he released me with one hand and ripped the wet satin scrap of underwear off of me. He thrust himself deep within and slid out ever so slowly. Viktor growled at me as he thrust in and out. "I am not my brother. I know what I want and I'm not afraid to take it." I should have been offended but the feel of him thrusting in and out rendered me senseless. At that point he could have said anything just as long as he kept going. I didn't want to make love I wanted to fuck and that's just what we did. When we were finally satiated we collapsed upon the lounging bed.

After our hearts slowed and we had recovered we swam in the glistening black pool. The water was warm and we played splashing and chasing each other and finally made love as leisurely as we had earlier been frantic.

Just before dawn he took me home and made sure I was safe. "Despite the interruptions this night has been the true beginning for us."

I wasn't sure how to react to that. I was deeply attracted to Viktor but I didn't want him getting the wrong idea.

"I definitely enjoyed myself tonight. I just don't want to mislead you. I don't want a relationship. Right now I just can't deal with the emotional stuff. I hope you understand. I love Tarik, I can't deal with him right now but we're not through." I waited to see his reaction. It sounded weird to me too now that I said it out loud. Yeah, that sounded good. I only want to use you for sex until I get back with the guy I actually care about.

"I know there is something between you and not just the bond of him turning you. Just know that I will never ask more than you can give. That doesn't mean I won't try and seduce you every day. It just means that I will respect your space."

I was relieved to hear that response but a little wary at the same time. Viktor always has an ulterior motive.

"Meet me tomorrow at the club. I want to start training you in hand to hand combat."

The sudden turn in conversation caught me off guard. I was glad he thought of it though. A few close calls had left me concerned about just that necessity.

"What time should I come by? He looked pleased that I hadn't argued.

"As early as you can make it. I'll be there at 10:00 myself."

"It's a date." I tiptoed up to kiss him goodnight and let myself in.

Chapter 21

Every night after hunting and feeding I met Viktor at the club to train. Each night I honed my skills in the gym there in the huge warehouse. Every night Viktor tried to seduce me. Tangling with him was such temptation it was inevitable that I would fall off the wagon. Maybe that was fall on because that is basically what happened. One particularly stupid move and I found myself pretty much impaled on him. Thirty seconds later we were skin to skin and in deep.

When I returned to the shop Skye was just leaving, "How was practice?"

She asked and I confessed my uncontrollable hormones had won again.

"I tripped and fell on his penis again. How can I be expected to show any restraint if he's going to walk around with that thing sticking out all of the time. It really was his fault."

"Oh, you poor thing I'm sure it was a terrible imposition for you. Next time just call me and I will help the poor guy out."

I decided that I had learned enough self defense now I needed to learn self preservation and stay away from Viktor.

I tried to get on with my life blocking all thoughts of Tarik and Viktor. Tarik had a connection with me that could never be broken. He was the vampire that made me and he could get inside my head at any time and the last week he had proven it. At the most embarrassing moment possible he could pop in and induce a mind blowing orgasm. He even zapped me once while training with Viktor. I pretended I was having a muscle cramp. This brought tele-porn to a whole new level.

Tarik was gunning for me with a full arsenal. He insisted on being at all my briefings and told me exactly how I would run each commission. By all means he was the bossiest boss I had ever had. Lately he was pushing me to expand to other cities and give lessons to other slayers on my techniques. Some jobs had gotten messy and I have begun carrying a squirt gun of holy water even when I wasn't on the job. That alone was very tricky to do. I had to bribe people into procuring the water and then donning heavy duty rubber gloves I had to carefully fill the gun. Even after filled the guns were dangerous because they tended to leak. My life was getting way too complicated. The only thing keeping me from quitting was the satisfaction of ridding the planet of these monsters.

The council was having a hard time weeding out the vamps who keep breeding newbies rampantly. By a rule of thumb each vampire only makes one new vampire every hundred years. Somewhere in Louisiana there was a group of vamps making far too many and it was up to me to help stop this. This also meant more time with both Viktor and Tarik who each took great joy in attempting to seduce me. I had just stormed out of a meeting with them and declared that I was done. "Just leave me alone!"

I needed a break. I returned to my life at the gallery and resumed work on the cemetery restoration. The money I donated had been enough to fund the restoration for years to come but the job was slow due to the lack of qualified preservationists. Every evening after I rose and fed and saw to the daily tedium of life I returned to Odd Fellows. Somehow it just felt like home there. I don't think it was just because that was where I was turned and where I rose. I felt the connection long before that, or the other pertinent event which I refuse to think about happened there.

Whenever I visited Odd Fellows Rest Daniel would appear and fill me in on the gossip and requests of the dead. I always kept a notebook in my backpack for just such occasions. It was filled with tons of interesting tidbits of information. The Marsalles twins wanted to know when the faceplate would be restored and both were badgering me as I wrote down all the facts. I sat cross legged upon the mound in the center of the cemetery and contemplated its history. Odd Fellows was built in 1847 and dedicated in 1849 when the first 16 Odd Fellows members' remains were brought here to rest from other cemeteries. The hearses carrying the remains were accompanied by circus cars and numerous members as the procession wound its way from Jackson Square through the city with a grand parade. I had heard the story from some of the original sixteen inhabitants and with each telling the procession sounded more elaborate like some kind of macabre fish story. The Odd Fellows were very proud ghosts and quick with their stories.

Odd Fellows had a charming and quite fitting opening but many cemeteries have fared much worse and still needed help with restoration and protection. Others like Girod Street cemetery opened in 1822 are no longer in existence. Named after the mayor of New Orleans the cemetery was deconsecrated and razed in 1957 and excavated in 1970 to make room for the Superdome parking garage. Hurray for progress! Maybe they should have asked some of its inhabitants what they thought. It's been nearly 40 years since most of the residents were moved and they are still pissed. Believe me I have heard the outrage. One famous Louisiana Circuit judge who died in a duel was particularly unhappy about his undignified re-burial in what he calls a mass grave. I hoped that my help could prevent such injustice from ever occurring again in New Orleans.

After most of my restoration projects finished I hoped to locate the former Girod cemetery residents and create a new special place for them. I just couldn't figure out how I would explain how I could tell which bones belong to which person. Daniel had proven he knew which bones were his but it might sound kind of kooky to say the ghosts told me. "I swear that's the Generals femur and the skull next to it belongs to his wife Emaline." But then again it is New Orleans and people here are used to living with the dead and not much surprises them. Everyone you meet can tell a ghost story or three. After such serious contemplation I got up to weed around Daniels grave and talked to him before taking the streetcar back home. It felt good to get away and think.

"Are you going to fix the squeaky gate on the Remaud's tomb? They keep bugging me about it." "I keep forgetting, I will bring the stuff next time I come, promise." "Great, they all bother me all the time cause they know you always come to see me. I think some of them are jealous you like me best." Daniel is such a cute little boy and I could detect the pride in his voice in being so important. When he was alive he was crippled and never taken seriously. Whenever I tried to talk to him about his life he clammed up and hid, sometimes for weeks.

"Yes, I'm afraid they're right. I do like you best. "

"How come none of the other vampires don't pay us no never mind? Most of them seem so uppity, like they're too good for us. They're dead too, just a different kind of dead."

I stifled a laugh at the way he described the others of my kind. I often wondered just the same thing. "From what Viktor told me they just don't like being reminded of what would have happened if they hadn't risen after dying. I think ghosts kind of scare them more than they do humans. You don't scare me though. Remember, I spoke to you and visited even before I could really see and hear you?"

Leslie Brown   79

"I remember, you did get scared that one time. You lit out of here like you was on fire. I never laughed so hard."

"That's not funny, I was really scared and afterward I thought I had offended you."

"I wasn't offended. I understand." He patted me on the shoulder and drifted off to his crypt.

I decided to walk home needing to release some energy and headed down Canal Street the couple of miles to my place. The night was lit by a full moon and with my vamp vision it seemed like day to me. I cut across to Basin street and headed to St Louis No. 1 cemetery. For some reason I felt drawn to the place. The gate was locked but I easily leapt the wall and landed on the other side without breaking a sweat. I listened for a while to see if I could tell what had drawn me. There were several black charcoal x's on Marie Laveau's tomb along with an odd assortment of offerings. I skirted a wide path around it since I had a bad experience with Voodoo before. I didn't want to accidently offend the queen of Voodoo.

I walked toward the back and stopped in front of a tomb I hadn't noticed before. The design on the front caught my eye. There was a tree carved into the marble and under it was the inscription;

For my beloved
Taken by treachery.
Reunited through immortality.
Damien Devereaux
1843-1870
Vivi Pierou
1849-1870

It was them, the reason for the curse. I was sure of it. This was the Voodoo priestess and her lover. Damien Devereaux, he had the same last name as me. Was it just a creepy coincidence or was our fate intertwined in more ways than just a curse? The tree that caught my eye was the one by our home in Texas. The inscription held no days but they had died in the same year. She must have died after twisting that terrible conjure that held my family for so many years. I felt a terrible chill behind me and turned reluctantly.

Deja Voodoo

The ghost of Marie Laveau stood before me. I recognized her from the many paintings I had seen all over town. "You weren't the only one to pay a price for dat curse. Vivi paid wit' her life and that of her unborn child." I looked at her terrified and unable to move. "Your family suffered but when a conjure of evil be done it returns three fold to the one who twist the curse. They suffered all these years souls separated at the crossroads waiting for you to fix this mess." I didn't know what to say. What could I say? Sorry it took so long? Sorry no one in my family had been smart enough to figure it out? Sorry that it had happened at all, that Damien had been murdered. It wasn't mine to be sorry for. Was Vivi sorry? Did she regret killing our mothers?

I remained silent, unsure of what to say. She moved closer to me and for the first time I was afraid of a ghost. What she said next surprised me.

"You been doin' some good work. The spirits tell me what you be doin' to help. Someone needs to speak for those that can't, protect those who need protecting." I finally broke my silence, "I'm just doing what's right." I took a deep breath and continued, "I am sorry that the curse ever happened. Sometimes things happen that we have no control over. I'm just glad it's over."

"No good came from that dark day. Tis' best if done wit' now maybe all those lost to this can rest peaceful like. You keep doin' what you been doin' and all that bad juju be forgotten someday." With that she disappeared and I was alone in the cemetery. I took one last look at Vivi and Damien's tom and left the way I had entered.

Chapter 22

When I got to the gallery it was closed and Sky had locked it hours earlier. Once inside I had a weird feeling though like I wasn't alone. Apparently this was my night for being creeped out, lucky me. I wasn't sure how much more my nerves could take. I whispered to Julie who appeared immediately which let me know something was really wrong. "Somebody's in my room- I mean in yo' room." She wrung her hands and paced the floor fading in and out. I pulled out my cell phone and speed dialed Viktor. "I have unwanted visitors in my bedroom. I'm going up."

"Don't you dare, be there in a minute I'm at Jackson Square wait for me." He hung up and I decided I would wait but only because he was close. The thought of a stranger in my room was intolerable. After the night I had I was not in the mood for more surprises.

I stood in the half open entry door and waited. Viktor was there in less than 2 minutes and he wasn't alone. Tarik was with him and we all went up the stairs together. Tarik led and I took up the rear. Who me? Chicken? Never! I'm the big bad vampire slayer. I just don't like to save all the fun for myself. We crept up quietly. Vampires give a new meaning to the word stealth. At the door we burst in to surprise the intruder.

He scrambled backward and fell on his butt. "Oh, shit!" He yelled and started explaining to the two vampires. "I'm not a burglar." I recognized his voice and came around Tarik to see for myself. "Don't hurt him! He's my brother in law," I yelled as I ran to throw myself between him and my protectors. "What the hell are you doing sneaking in here and not telling me you were coming? Where are Alex and the baby?"

"They're at home." I took a minute to look at him and then I realized he had changed. Luke was now one of us. Alex had turned him. We had talked about just this scenario. They had agreed to leave him human to pursue his snowboarding career. Alex didn't like it though and was worried he would get killed. Apparently she had gotten tired of worrying. "She did it. She didn't even talk to me she just attacked me and did it. I can't fucking believe this. I can't ever compete again. I came here to see if there is a cure. Can you switch me back?" Tarik and Viktor both started laughing and teasing him. "Poor little pup he wants his life back." I aimed two well placed elbows and jabbed them each in the ribs. "That's enough; I can handle this from here. Thanks for rushing to my rescue but you can both leave now."

After they retreated I made Luke sit down and explain everything. Apparently there was a horrible accident and his best friend had died on the mountain. They had switched jackets just before the incident so when the body was retrieved everyone thought it was Luke but he was still on the mountain crest and didn't know what happened. When she found out Alex was furious and turned him immediately. Luke had come here right after rising to get help. Unfortunately vampirism isn't reversible. The best I could do was calm him down and give him a place to stay until he cooled off. I taught him to hunt and protect himself like I had been taught and assured Alex all would be well. She was a little bit sorry for rushing to do what she had but also felt they were better off this way.

Luke was a happy vampire when he found out that there was a whole vampire world of sports. They compete at night all over the world from skiing to Wakeboarding and he was good to go when we introduced him to the right people and set up his first competition. Alex came to retrieve her runaway groom and we spent a week together. The baby was growing so much. The terrible two's were taking up residence in Stacia's baby brain. She gets into everything! When they left I missed tripping over her toys and her bright smile.

Chapter 23

It was time to get back to work. Viktor was insistent that I help him with some cases. Tarik had gone out of state to other regions on council matters. We were getting near to the source of the infestation of new vamps. Through some surveillance we had been able to rid the city of a number of bad guys. It just takes a few of them to make it hard for the regular vampires. We didn't need supernatural drug dealers or worse. There were plenty of those in human form to go around. Every time I had a meal off the hoof so to speak I tried to pick those kinds of people. I used my mind tricks to rehab them and felt that even if I was using them at least I was trying to make them better people.

I was doing surveillance on a target and had to spend a lot of time in the clubs, posing as a new vamp and had gotten in with their clique. By keeping my ears open I was finding out names and places. My target was pretty high up on the food chain and I had a "date" planed with him. He was one of the bastards that turned children and women to make them sex slaves.

So far all my commissions had been fairly easy. Except for fending off roving hands and tongues I had very few problems.

This guy was a different story though. I led the target to my house and realized right away he was trouble. He grabbed me by the hair and threw me to the floor when we entered the house. At first I thought my cover was blown but soon I realized he was just a bastard. He liked to beat his women. It would be a pleasure putting him out of my misery. I got up and faced him. "So you like to play rough?" He grinned and came at me grabbing my shoulders and kissing me brutally. I pulled away and said, "Then let's play". I led him to the toy room and motioned for him to look around. The walls were full of great playthings and I saw his eyes light up. He grabbed me again and I thought I wouldn't be able to get away. Finally he gave me an opening and I slapped him hard. Apparently he could dish it out but he couldn't take it. The anger in his eyes spurred me to run and I just barely made it to the door and pushed the button. His hand was caught in the door and was sliced off cleanly by the force of the electronic sealing mechanism and I dove to shield myself from the rays of light. "You fucking bitch!" His screams echoed in the house but died as quickly as he did.

I watched his severed hand turned to ash and his keys had melted so clean up was tricky. Viktor and I talked and decided that I needed a new bag of tricks. Word was getting out and the vamps had figured out that a female vamp was luring them away. My disguises were wearing thin and I was getting burnt out. Meanwhile Viktor was trying to heat things up again. I wasn't sure where I stood with Tarik and I was still mad at him. Here I was a twenty eight year old vampire who had managed to have sex twice in the first year, the first time in a cemetery and the second time in a hearse. What does that say about me? I talk to the dead more than the living and I had not painted for months. I decided it was time to quit trying to please everyone else and just do what I wanted to do.

Chapter 24

After the gallery closed I went with Skye and some friends to hear a new band. We had been doing more things together and she was used to my odd hours. She had been doing some cerebral acrobatics and had declared that she knew I was a vampire. Not only did she believe that I was one but she decided that Tarik and Viktor were as well. I finally confessed and swore her to secrecy. We spent more time together and I finally had someone I could talk to about everything.

"You really should just suck it up and make nice with Tarik," Sky insisted daily. I think she leaned towards him mainly because she still had a major crush on Viktor. "So he abandoned you once. He came back and he is interested. Just tell him why you had to make him turn you. Surely then he will understand?"

I guess I was just stubborn but I couldn't do that. He was wrong and he owed me an apology. Until then I intended to just live my life. The two sexy vampires could just rot. I avoided them both and started getting on with my life.

There is something so liberating about not letting a man interfere in your life. I started painting again and was specializing in vampire portraits now. Tarik and Viktor weren't the only bloodsuckers in the piranha bowl. This town was dripping in hot vamps. Having your portrait painted by me was becoming the in thing to do for their crowd. It wasn't like they could go down to the Wal Mart portrait studio for the $19.99 special. As a lot we are somewhat vain and love seeing ourselves since mirrors weren't an option paintings were popular. I was getting especially good at the female vamps. The business was growing and I had purchased the building next door to house the portrait gallery which we named Fangtastic Illusions. The cover was that anyone could have a vampire portrait, I had even tried a few lycans. The humans just thought it was a unique form of art and I painted them to match their Fantasies.

Business was booming and we had hired 3 more employees, all of which were in on the whole vampire scene. One was a daytime guard for the gallery space. The sculptures Skye was creating were selling faster than ever and she could barely keep up. She no longer worked in the gallery except to relieve someone. She was also starting to bug me about making her a vamp. I told her it was against the rules. We were under a strict 100 year limit. I told her I would find someone who was willing to donate their quota and she let it rest. I knew that my soul was intact and had no fear that becoming a vampire took that from you. I also believed the ghosts were just the souls of people separated from their bodies. I wasn't sure how the holy water burned us though. So much of this existence is just speculation.

Chapter 25

My thoughts were interrupted by Julie the ghost wandering in and out of the room ranting about stubborn men. Her lover had apparently told her to spend one night on the roof naked and he would marry her. That was the night she had frozen to death and he was too caught up in a card game to realize she had taken him seriously. Ever since then she haunted the rooms and he haunted the porch. Neither would give in and go talk to the other so I had become their go between.

"Could you please put on some clothes?" Julie never seemed to realize she was naked unless I brought it up.

"Sorry, I was just so mad at that miserable excuse of a man I forgot. Why are you so hung up on clothes anyway? It's just us girls here." She instantly became fully clothed in an elaborate gown that looked like it was out of Gone with the Wind. Julie had been pampered and always given the finest things by her French lover. He simply refused to marry her and that tiny thing kept them apart even in death. In their time it was against the law in the United States for a person of color no matter how little the percentage to marry a white person. Julie had begged him to take her to France where they could legally wed. Apparently he had commitment issues.

I hoped I could help with that matter now. "Julie, did you know that it is legal now to marry anyone you want no matter what color they are?"

She looked at me suspiciously and crossed her arms while tapping her foot, a sure sign of agitation with her. "It's true. The laws say that everyone must be treated equally no matter what race, sex, or religion. It's even legal in some states to marry the same sex."

"You can't be serious!" Julie burst out laughing and held her belly as she rolled onto the couch.

"I'm not fooling you, it's true. If you wanted you could marry anyone. Or at least anyone who is also dead, and willing to marry you, and the priest would also have to be dead. It would work though. We could have a whole ghost wedding. It would be fun. We could do it at night in here."

I thought Julie would be ecstatic but she just deflated more.

"It doesn't matter if it's legal he still won't marry me. I don't even think he loves me". She nodded toward the balcony where her lover sat drinking his imaginary absinthe and glaring at the tourists.

Deja Voodoo

"I will talk to him. Just leave all the details up to me". Julie disappeared as I left the room and stepped out on the balcony. I had the same conversation over again and with his consent I set off to make arrangements. The person or ghost shall I say that I needed to see was just around the corner from here. Pere Antoine was a priest who had served at Jackson Cathedral in his time. He usually hung out at the alley beside the cathedral named after him. I found him in the garden between Pirates Alley and his own namesake, Pere Antoine's Alley. He was trying to talk two angry men out of a duel. In the hours before dawn I often saw the duels being perpetually re-enacted. It was all quite pointless to me. They were dead. Killing each other again seemed, well, overkill.

"Pere Antoine" I called out in hopes of drawing him away from the other ghosts. He looked my way but pretended to not see me. It's kind of like the humans who see and hear ghosts but refuse to acknowledge them. It's just rude! I stalked up to him and stood between the two idiots trying to kill each other again.

"Look! You're already dead! You can't kill each other again what would be the point?" They just looked sheepish and slowly disappeared. That left me alone with the priest. And he didn't look too happy to see me. Maybe it was the whole undead, soulless, going to hell sort of discrimination. I wasn't so sure I bought into all of that. It didn't feel like I was soulless. I faced him squarely, hands on hips ready for a fight. In my experience some of the church people were the deepest in denial. I had my own theories there. Jesus did rise three days after death too. I didn't figure I was in such bad company. My rule was, don't do anything you're ashamed of and protect those weaker than you. I figure there are a lot worse things out there than just a vampire.

"I need your help. Please don't ignore me I know you can see me. I am not evil, just dead and it looks like you're in the same boat so please listen." He stopped his retreat and turned back to me.

"What makes you believe I think you're evil? You don't even know me. You might be surprised."

"I'm sorry. I just thought that since I am a vampire you would shun me."

"It's not for me to judge you."

Leslie Brown   89

"Oh, well then maybe you could help me?"

He looked skeptical but I took his silence as a chance to explain.

"I live down the street and the ghosts in my house want to get married. When she was alive interracial marriages were illegal but now they are not. Can you perform a ceremony for them?"

"Well, that's not exactly what I would think a vampire would ask me. You must be as unusual as they say."

"Who and what is it they say?"

"Everyone's talking about the vampire that helps the ghosts. They say you are restoring their graves and helping them to come to terms with their issues. Apparently it's true. Here you are playing matchmaker to the dead."

"O.K. so does that mean you will help me?"

"Of course I will help. I do not know that the ceremony will be legally binding and all that but I will do my best."

We set up arrangements and I went home to tell Julie. She exploded into a whirlwind of activity to get ready for the big day. She actually went out on the balcony and jerked her soon to be husband out of his drunken stupor to tell him the news. He looked quite relieved and quit drinking all night long. Things were looking up at least for this couple. I on the other hand was as lonely as ever.

Tarik was entering my dreams more than ever and kept insisting we could be lovers. I told him in no uncertain terms that I would not be a casual fling for him. He was still convinced that I had changed and accused me of sleeping with Viktor, which of course I had so there was no point in denying it. I was getting so tired of the confusion I threw it in his face. "Just admit it you were wrong to leave me like you did."

"I was not wrong; being a vampire has changed you.
"No it hasn't. I just have more resources available to me to do the things I would have done on a much smaller scale."
"You never would have become a killer!"

"It's not killing if they are already dead!"

With that I walked away.

Chapter 26

It was Halloween and that time of year made me feel quite melancholy since it was the time I had changed and the only time I had been with Tarik. I was in the cemetery late one evening after feeding on a fat bastard child predator. They taste like shit but the satisfaction of getting another one off the streets is worth it. My skills were becoming finely honed and I instilled in them a feeling of violent nausea in the presence of children. That insured an inability for them to continue their heinous crimes. Other vampires thought I was a wimp for not just killing them but I couldn't do that. I could be judge and executioner but only if they were already dead. I left the live ones up to their own fate with a little rehab for good measure.

I was popping a mint into my mouth to get the foul taste of the molester out when Tarik showed up. He just flew into the fenced area, very Mary Poppin's but faster. In a few more years I should be able to do the same.

"Don't start with me now. I'm not in the mood."

"Sorry, I just felt that you were very disturbed. I wanted to make sure you were okay." He kept his distance from me which was probably a good thing. He looked like sex and candy all wrapped up in a shiny bow. Tonight I was feeling too weird to deal with his theatrics and teasing. I wanted him more than anything and I didn't trust myself this close to him. He thought we could just be casual that it meant nothing. I couldn't lock away my feelings like that.

I could do casual, just not with him. For me it was way too big of a wound to heal. He just left me without even giving me a chance to explain. Now it didn't matter. I hadn't changed but he refused to see it. Well maybe I changed a little, bloodsucking vampires be damned. Inside I was basically the same person.

He watched all the emotions play across my face as I watched his unreadable one. There was so much I didn't know about Tarik, I didn't even know how old he was, 200, 300, 400?

"It doesn't matter."

He had read my mind and I snapped out of my brooding.

"Stop doing that!" I jabbed him in the chest with a finger at each word for emphasis.

"I am not yours to invade anytime you want. Just because you turned me does not give you the right, and stop with the tele-porn. Enough already! I am not going to be your booty call girl. You had your chance with me."

"I came here to apologize. I spoke to Viktor and he finally told me why you kept secrets from me. I understand now and I am here to make it up to you."

He stood there like he expected me to hump his leg in joy.

"Oh sure, the high and mighty vampire ruler had deigned to forgive me! I guess I should bow down and grovel now. My clothes should just melt off and I sacrifice myself to you again? Not! I've had enough of your shit! You forgive me? I don't forgive you! You should have had some faith. Now it's too late, and I'm over you!"

That was so not true but I wasn't going to confess. He could just eat his heart out. I left him there to digest that bit of information.

As I walked home my steps became lighter. I felt better than I had in months. It was wonderful telling him off and standing up for myself. I don't know if he was giving me my space or if I was getting better at blocking his intrusion but he quit entering my mind. I had a Halloween party/wedding to arrange and I was feeling free finally.

Chapter 27

Halloween was always my favorite holiday. Since I had it out with Tarik I felt more like my old self and was really looking forward to the event. Every day people tell their kids "don't take candy from strangers" and one night a year you dress them up and send them out begging for candy from those same strangers, go figure. My sister and I had always made our own costumes and planned parties' months ahead of time. For me the dressing up in costumes was my favorite thing. Alex just loved the candy and of course every year had to be a witch. Each year her costumes were different. Sometimes Alex was a good witch, other times she was a bad witch. Our dad was always there to make sure we were safe and it was just fun.

My party was going to be the event of the town, excluding the vampire ball and other than Mardi Gras, not to mention the other thousand occaisions. New Orleans is just a party town. Tonight I was heading to the Anne Rice, Vampire Lestat Vampire Ball. My first night out free and unencumbered by vacillating boyfriends or the fear of intimacy due to impending motherhood and subsequent death. That problem was gone forever and I was ready to live or whatever you do when you're dead or undead, whatever. I was ready to party.

Skye and I arrived at the ball in a limo both dressed to the nines. She had outdone herself with my hair and it was twisted and shaped into an obscenely high coiffure. My dress, yes I said dress was cut up to here and down to there. I let it all hang out, at least the fangs anyway. It was a vampire ball after all. Half of the fangs in the room were real.

The performers were outstanding and I was so happy to see my favorite singer Dilana who used to live in Houston. I love the Voodoo doll song she sings and my all time favorite is Supersoul. Voltaire was there again and just as sexy as ever. His soul tortures tunes just hit your heart. Anne Rice left a video message to her fans and wished them well. Since moving to California after the death of her husband Stan she no longer attended the ball. The party was a fundraiser for Habitat New Orleans. I donated a vampire portrait of Lestat this year which brought an obscene amount of money.

I was at the bar getting a drink, not what you think. Vampires can eat and drink moderately. The older the vamp the less tolerable though. I had a glass of red wine and gave my feet a rest from all the dancing and obnoxiously high heels.

The mirror behind the bar was draped in black, not that it mattered and I didn't see him approach but I felt the presence of a vampire. No big surprise but I was still on guard. I turned as he approached unable to leave my back open to any danger. I'd fried enough bad ones to know there were many in that category.

Deja Voodoo

He took the seat next to me and I tried to watch him without staring. He was quite yummy, another tall, dead and sexy guy. My night was definitely looking up. I turned full on to him and smiled with all my teeth. I hoped it didn't look like a growl. Even dead people have insecurities. He wasn't terrified apparently because he stayed right there. The vampire wore a deep ultramarine blue waistcoat with black velvet lapels and breeches which were tucked into tall pirate boots. His hair was black, shoulder length and shaggy chic topped with a hat probably stolen from Jean Lafitte himself. The most astounding thing though was the color of his eyes. They were a piercing blue that matched the coat ringed by a lighter blue and then black. I had never seen eyes like that. They were odd like a birds eyes, watching and unreadable.

"This party is dead do you want to get out of here." He grinned at me and I couldn't help but grin back at his pun.

"My coffin or yours?"

He laughed appropriately at my dorky joke and offered his hand.

"I'm Terry, short for Terrance."

"I'm Kat, Katrina. Nice to meet you, I've never seen you at any of these events are you from here?"

"It's been a while but this is my home. I was born in New Orleans."

"Well it's definitely been a pleasure meeting you but I came with a friend and I don't want to abandon her."

"You mean the one sneaking out the back door with the guy that has more tattoos than a Seurat has dots?"

"That just figures, I can't compete with those tattoos, I'm just her boss and best friend. She better not expect a Christmas bonus."

I was impressed that he knew who Seurat was let alone that he painted using dots formally known as pointillism.

"Are you trying to impress me with your artistic knowledge?"

"Of course not, If I was trying to impress you with my artistic knowledge I would have mentioned that he was a friend of mine. My nephew Edgar introduced us. You might have heard of him he painted some very pretty dancers."

My jaw dropped and he gently closed it for me.

"You're Edgar Degas Uncle? I knew he had family here but I never dreamed they were still around, at least not the family that actually knew him, ancestors surely. I am definitely impressed. Did you know Van Gogh as well? Don't answer my heart couldn't take it."

I watched him over the rim of my wine glass. Sexy, cultured, did I mention sexy. He was just what the doctor ordered.

"I do believe I will take you up on your offer. Let's get out of here." My limo was nearby and we took it to the French Quarter where we walked and talked until almost dawn. We were on the walk by the Mississippi when we finally admitted that it was time to part. I was having the best time and didn't want it to end. I liked Terry, short for Terrence which he made me swear an oath never to call him.

He pulled me into his arms and I expected a gentle kiss goodnight but it was anything but gentle. I was stunned by the impact of my desire. I barely knew this man and I was ready to crawl right down his throat, definitely yummy. We kissed and I broke it off reluctantly. Dawn was near and I was in danger either way. I left him at the river and got home just in time to fall into a dead sleep. My last thought was that I hoped he made it home before dawn. It would be a shame to fry such a fine specimen.

Chapter 28

The wedding was all set and the bride was proving to be a real bridezilla. She kept changing her dress and yelling at the bridesmaids. I left them upstairs to check on the preparations downstairs. Everything was decorated for Halloween downstairs and the wedding upstairs. The party looked to be quite interesting. The guest list included vampires, lycanthropes, ghosts, and humans. The one guest I was most interested in was Terry. I had invited him and felt sure we had a connection but a girl never knows.

Deja Voodoo

Before the Halloween guests arrived the ghosts came for the nuptials. It was oddly like a human wedding with the same hideous bridesmaids' dresses and the same vows said except for the death do you part stuff, kind of unnecessary under the circumstances. Even though most of the guests and the entire wedding party were translucent the wedding was beautiful. I had the bride's favorite flowers, gardenias everywhere and the house smelled divine. Julie finally settled on an off the shoulder gown with delicate beadwork and embroidery.

When the ceremony was over there was no cake or photographs just everyone wishing the happy couple well and then disappearing. The newly wedded couple faded off and I wondered if we would ever see them again. I thanked Pere Antoine and promised to leave a donation at the church. He had presided over Jackson cathedral for many years and was the most beloved priest of all time. The current cathedral was built entirely on donations from one gentleman, the only non clergy buried within the church along with Pere Antoine.

The Halloween party guests were beginning to arrive as I joined them downstairs. Skye had been holding down the fort. She couldn't see the ghosts so it was pointless to attend the wedding. A few vampires had attended and they followed me down to the party. I had finally gotten some of the vampires to start treating the ghosts with more respect instead of ignoring them. It's kind of sad when you are ignored all the time or when people just plain can't see you. Before turning I was able to see a few ghosts but not nearly as clear as now. Before I was turned they just appeared in my peripheral vision or as shadows. From the moment I stepped out of that tomb I could see them as clear as live humans. The same became true with other things like I can tell a lycanthrope from human any day. Zombies never get past me anymore, and ghouls, don't even go there!

I slipped out to don my costume quickly. It was kind of weird but I had decided to go as a Voodoo doll. I twisted my hair up and had added colorful extensions just for this occasion. Sky helped me tie on the costume and threw on some quick makeup. I greeted the rest of the guests standing with my feet together and my arms out straight. I even had a few pins sewed in to look like they were sticking me. Mama JoJo and I were again on speaking terms and she just loved the costume. When I had finally given up my post at the door Terry showed up. I tried not to look desperate and greeted him coolly. He was wearing jeans and a t-shirt. Terry flashed his fangs at me and said "this is my costume". He looked me up and down.

"Yours is better though. I especially love what you have done to your hair." He seemed sincere so I let it slide that he had arrived so late.

"I'm glad you came, let me show you around the galleries." We walked arm in arm throughout the rooms and he declared his undying adoration of my work.

"You will have to come to my home and see my private collection. I have several paintings by Edgar that have never been shown outside of a few close friends."

"That sounds very familiar. Hmm, come in and let me show you my etchings?"

"No, no I didn't mean it like that. I just thought since you are an artist you might be interested."

"Of course I'm interested, I was just kidding. I would love to see the paintings. I always loved his work especially the little girl in the dance studio." I remembered when I studied Degas in college and learned that he was commissioned to go and paint some ballet dancers. He was quite pissed and to just be obtuse he painted the lead dancers frumpy younger sister instead. Some of the paintings he created from that time became his most famous".

"I am ready to see them any time just say the word."

"Alright then it's a date. Tomorrow night if you don't have plans already?" I pretended to think about it for a while and then conceded to him.

"I think I can rearrange some things and fit you in tomorrow night. Pick me up at eleven? I have work to do earlier in the evening."

"I will count the minutes." Terry bowed over my hand and mocked my own teasing manner. He grabbed one of the pins out of my costume and did a fake stab in his heart and writhed in agony before me. "I am yours to command."

He was so fun to be with, such a difference from the intense vampires who I refuse to name. Terry is fun and goofy and cute and he likes art obviously.

We were alone in an alcove by some of my newest vamp paintings so I tugged at his t-shirt to pull him closer. My new outlook on life had me feeling bold and I kissed him though with less intensity than the night before. He was just a little bit taller than me and for once I didn't have to strain to meet up with a man. My hands strayed to his dark messy curls and toyed with the ends that barely reached his shoulder blades. The tousled look really worked for him. Did I mention he has blue eyes? I had always been a sucker for blue eyes and black hair. No pun intended.

Terry was built like someone who works hard for a living and not at a desk. The t-shirt showed off his muscles and I was thankful to whoever had invented the garment. I suppose he had been built that way before being turned because our body shapes change very little. All the little scars and blemishes heal but we don't change all that drastically. Vampires just become a little more perfected. My hair for instance, when I was human it was completely unmanageable but now, every day is a good hair day. The color is more vibrant and the curls are always perfect. If I could sell vampire hair in a bottle I would be a millionaire. Terry was winding his fingers in my hair and pulling me deeper into his embrace. I reluctantly pulled back. I was hosting a party and it might seem a little gauche to ride him like a grocery store horsey right then and there.

"I really hate to do this but I need to mingle." His full lips pouted and made me almost give in. Man this guy really did it for me. I would have to be very careful with such a distraction.

"I'll just leave you to your guests and wait until tomorrow. I am a patient man. For your 150th birthday it is a law that you are finally awarded patience. Lucky for me you're not that old yet."

If his sheepish grin didn't make it all better I might have been offended. He kissed my cheek and left me with my guests.

I had definitely been ignoring them and turned my attention where it was needed, potential customers. John Blake, the mayor and hopeful governor if the next election went his way who was a vampire wanted his wife's portrait made. We talked and I showed them several portraits getting ideas from them. She is also a vampire and previously a supermodel so of course I just wanted to hate her instantly! Luckily she's not a bitch and actually has a brain or I wouldn't even consider painting her nails let alone her portrait.

Many of the ghosts stayed after the wedding and I noticed they were mingling well with the vampires. Some of my human friends were even starting to open up to them and could also interact with the ghosts. I figured it would be months before Julie let her man up for air so I didn't expect to see her when I did.

"I just wanted to thank you for what you did for me." She spoke quickly and then vanished again.

That is so like Julie, making a hit and run compliment." I smiled and gave myself a mental cookie for my good deed. "Good vampire."

"Do you always talk to yourself?"

I rounded the corner and my head smacked into the chest that was speaking to me. I looked up and it was Tarik. I didn't know he was even at the party and was unable to think fast.

"Huh?" Yeah, quite witty I know. Way to look cool. I recovered enough to question him.

"Do you always crash parties or just mine?"

He looked like he was thinking about it. "Just yours." The stairway was small and he would have to move for me to continue down and around the corner. He did not look like he was going to move.

"Love the costume, how did you find a horses ass big enough? Oh, I'm sorry that's not a costume?"

"How long are you going to be mad at me? I'm not the one who's screwing with your head. Do you even know who you were face to face with earlier?"

He must have seen me with Terry, it served the smug bastard right. He thinks he can tell me what to do. "I know exactly who he is. He's the guy who doesn't run off and leave me and then come back and order me around like a dog." That felt good. "As a matter of fact we are having what you might call a RELATIONSHIP. It's one of those things where two people meet and they get to know each other and don't lie about being the head of the vampire council. You know, where one person sticks around to hear what the other has to say. And by the way why were you really locked in that coffin?"

He ignored my question and badgered me some more. "Before you get too deep you better find out about him, he's dangerous. I just don't want you getting hurt."

"Are you referring to the fact that he is a mercenary?"

"That and some other things, there's more to him than just the art dealer façade. You're too different."

"We're different? What could we possibly have in common? Oh, I don't know, maybe it's the art thing? Oh no, I know it's the killing thing, or that were both dead? Duh, I could have had a V8!"

I probably looked ridiculous ranting at him dressed up like a voodoo doll but I was pissed. He had no right to interfere. He also had no right looking like he did it just wasn't fair. His hair was tied back and I just wanted to yank out the band holding it and ravish him right there on the stairs. Vampire hormones just suck!

"I need some breathing room maybe I'll be over my mad in about 100 years. See you then." I turned and went back the way I came. As soon as I left him I wanted desperately to run back and throw myself at him, if I did that though he would always walk all over me. Tarik was way powerful and stubborn. If I ever wanted a chance of a relationship with him I would have to stand up to him.

Close to dawn the party dissipated and all the little ghouls went home to their coffins and attics. I just laid my head down when I got a little instant message in my brain from Terry. This vampire telepathy sure helped keep the cell phone bill down.

"I can't wait to see you."

"Me too, I really like spending time with you. See you tomorrow."

Chapter 29

I smiled as I woke up and stretched as I left my little daybed in my safe room. Tonight I was meeting Terry but I had a few hours before then and a rat to feed from. I dressed in my super soft faded, torn jeans, black boots and t-shirt. Who needs a bra when you're permanently perky? I strapped on a belt with a can of compressed holy water. I had found that easier to control than the squirt guns. Viktor had taken my idea and was having them specially made for us. He was also working on a way to use the light rays as a mobile weapon. Just for measure I slid some silver bladed knifes into my boot and my Super-mace pockets. Super-mace is special formula for weres. I assume it has the equivalent to saying to a dog, "do you want a bath?" The little varmints run like hell when they see it. I had taken self defense lessons from Viktor and was getting quite good with the knife.

One evening while I was coming home, cutting across Rampart and down to Bourbon Street I had stopped to talk to a local. He was a local grifter but essentially harmless. Guys like him just tried to make a buck off of street scams. I figure if you're stupid enough to fall for that crap then you pretty much deserve it. When a stranger stops you and tries to make a bet, beware.

At the Blacksmith's shop some well meaning tourist saw the poor little white girl bothered by the big scary black dude and offered assistance. It annoyed me so much I just turned and bared my fangs at him. He took off running like the Devil was after him. I had to chase him down and do some mind tricks to erase that memory. Since then I was more careful.

I walked into the Blacksmith shop and took a stool at the bar and ordered a Bloody Mary. I had only been dead a few years and could still tolerate some food and drinks. The day I am no longer able to enjoy a Bloody Mary or a pizza will be sad indeed. The bartender was a girl named Tina who also happened to be a werewolf. There were more werewolves in New Orleans than any other species. The swamp legends of the Loup Gareau are not far off. The biker bar just off Bourbon Street was owned by werewolves. There were also a lot of wererats and wereravens here and a few weregators. Those are just freaking scary. Anytime you need information though see Tina.

I had heard that there was a wererat involved in the child porn industry. Tina had been getting some information for me to help find him. I suspect that she had reason to hate perverts like him since she sought me out with the information and had helped in similar cases before. She managed to lure him to the Blacksmith's shop for me. He sat in the corner looking around warily.

The ghost of Jean Lafitte, the pirate sat down beside me and I motioned for him to ignore me. I made eyes at the lowlife and Lafitte took the cue. He just sat there and drank his ale. Normally I would have a beer and listen to Lafitte's stories but I had a job to do. The wererat had been told he would meet a supplier here and he kept looking at his watch. The dial glowed every time he pushed the button in the dim bar. The only light came from a few candles and a some lighted signs behind the bar. The bar was the oldest one in America and was not made for electricity. At night it's darker inside the bar than on the street. A carriage pulled up to the corner with tourists being told the story of the Blacksmith's Shop and offered a drink from Tina who provides curbside service for lucrative tips. It's amazing how people will tip when the girl is such a doll.

I continued to watch the were as he downed the last of his third beer. Finally the rat gave up at around 10 p.m. and left the bar. I followed him down Bourbon and hid in the crowds. When I had my chance I dove into a crowd for camouflage and I got ahead of him. I waited in a doorway that led to a courtyard. Were's are very strong and I would have to be careful and fast. I reached for the knife and held it ready. When the Were came by I grabbed him and held the blade to his heart while I sank my fangs into his neck. I found that draining the really bad guys was the easiest way to weaken them and then I could cut out the heart. I had also learned that getting most of the blood out first made it not so icky. These are my favorite jeans and I do have a date after all.

All finished up and not a drop on me. Viktor had been tailing me and his men moved in for the clean up. Some nights it was just too easy. I just wish the bad guys didn't taste so foul. I popped in a handful of breath mints to kill the aftertaste of scumbag, a very poor vintage indeed. Anyway, like I said I had a date. I turned down Dumaine and headed toward Royal. Just as I got there Terry arrived at my door.

"What's a scary guy like you doing lurking around my door?"

"I'm scary? What nefarious deed have you been up to so early in the evening?"

"I could tell you but you know..."

We hugged and walked off chattering about nothing important. His home was on Esplanade, several blocks away near City Park but the walk gave us time to talk. I told him about my rat job and he told me about a mass murderer he had finally gotten enough intel on to eliminate. Terry is like me he doesn't mind the dirty work but he chooses the targets. We don't do disgruntled partners or spurned lovers. We consider ourselves societies cleanup crew and the pay was good. Soon I would have enough money to restore some dignity to the poor souls from Girod street cemetery. There's nothing like having your eternal resting place bulldozed. How rude is that?

We walked along Esplanade in the neutral ground between the two sides of the road under the many towering trees. The moon was full and with the vamp vision thing we could see like it was daylight. Interspersed between rambling mansions both restored and dilapidated were empty lots and the occasional businesses as well as several schools. At the end of the street where the park begins is the museum. Some of these homes had been damaged during the hurricane but most were getting back to normal. We held hands and Terry pointed out the landmarks as we passed by them. Soon we arrived at his home. This was not the original home that Edgar had visited but a newly restored and much larger one. The original home was now a hotel.

Like my home Terry's housed a small gallery downstairs but his was not open to the public. The massive porch welcomed you with its bright white paint and beveled glass windows. It was just too pretty to be a guys place. Inside was no different it looked more like a museum. I recognized several priceless works by the impressionists which definitely impressed me. We entered a locked room where I presumed the secret paintings were hidden.

They were incredible. These paintings were the ones I preferred. They were from the racetracks where Edgar often painted while in New Orleans. The race track is just up the street from the original Degas house. The race track is the home to the New Orleans Jazz Festival. People don't realize how big City Park is, over 1300 acres. There is a stable, and the park was once a plantation along Bayou St. John where Marie Laveau held rituals. Some of the trees are over 600 years old.

I admired the racing paintings taking a moment to study each one. Horses were always my favorite animals. I was definitely not a Ballet kind of girl but even those works fascinated me. Terry allowed me time to study the paintings and pretended to not notice the tears that welled up.

We left the room and ascended the staircase to the area that Terry lived in. Like my home the living quarters were divided among the upper floors. We went out to sit on the banquette-balcony if you're not Creole. There was a comfy wicker couch that we nestled into. It felt so good to not be pushed to rush things. I felt more comfortable with Terry than anyone but my sister.

We were becoming very close friends but I just didn't want it to go any further than that right now. I had enough to deal with in that department.

Chapter 30

Terry and I hung out together often and my day to day life was very busy. We had kept it low key so far, he was fun to be with and kissed divinely but I was taking this slow. I had more orders for portraits than a vampire can sink her teeth into. One day I pulled out one of the original portraits of Tarik to study it. It looked more alive to me than the other ones I have painted. I guess that was because my heart was really in it. The painting showed him propped up in bed with the covers sliding around his waist. He was leaning forward, willing the viewer to him with his eyes. The long dark cascade of hair framed him so that the whiteness of his skin glowed. I don't think it is just how yummy he looks though that draws me in. There is something in his soul that calls to me through the paint.

From the moment he entered my dreams he was embedded in my being. When you know you are connected to someone so deeply you feel powerless. Tarik had been powerful as a human but as a long dead vampire he was much stronger. I would have to be strong to survive with him. I set the painting back and decided to make some changes. I had a growing business, more money than I could count thanks to my "special services," and needed some space. With a little time on the internet I found several pieces of property for sale.

I told Skye to hold down the fort and I started out to look at some of the ones I had marked. The first was in the Garden District and it was nice but it just wasn't me. The second was in the Warehouse district. The place had a cool industrial chic vibe but it was way too close to Viktor. Finally against my better judgment I looked at a place on Canal Street. I thought it would be too busy but as I drove I realized it was near the end of the street by the cemeteries. I fell in love instantly.

I bought the building on Canal Street to make my new home and studio. Most people would be freaked out but the architecture and size as well as location of the building drew me to the old mortuary. What did I have to fear, I was already dead? The 14,000 square foot mortuary was built in the mid 1872 by Mary Slattery and after the second owner sold it in 1923 when it became McMahon's Mortuary and needed renovation. When used as a mortuary over 20,000 upscale services were performed. The front faces Canal Street with its towering white columns and impressive entry. There are cemeteries next door, behind, and across the street all the way to the end at City Park Street. Odd Fellows is on the corner and I can actually see inside its' walls from the third floor. From the upper floors you get a spooky bird's eye view of the cemeteries.

I planned for the top floor to be my new studio and the second floor for living area. The entrance was elevated and the lower floor felt like a basement but was actually on ground level. The whole city is below sea level so basements are not an option. The bottom floor had ample room to install a "panic room" complete with security monitors showing every room and all

Leslie Brown

entrances. The builders didn't need to know that is really my daytime resting space. With a lot of rushing the renovations will be finished for Mardi Gras when my sister and her family plan to visit.

Skye was moving into my old apartment above the gallery and the offices and storage areas downstairs were being converted to new gallery space. There was plenty of room at the mortuary for offices and storage. I moved into the mansion a month before Mardi Gras and was happy to be out of the French Quarter. It was odd having so much space to myself and being able to work without being confined. My paintings are rather large and by the time I frame them they are huge. The supplies for the frames can take up massive amounts of space as well.

The location of my new home turned out to be perfect. Nearby there is an architectural antique warehouse that I can find most of the things I need to create my custom made frames. From broken chandeliers to broken paned windows the supply was endless. I bought everything that took my fancy. I had plenty of room in the attic which was a treasure trove all by itself.

When it came to making my frames I could rummage around and find just the perfect combination of things to compliment the painting. I had a heavy duty vent put in a small room to make it a perfect space for spray painting. In the attic of the mausoleum there was an endless supply of broken furniture. Table and chair legs were a staple for my creations so I was as happy as a vampire at a blood bank. It was just as I was rummaging for some items when I met the first ghost there. He was a little bit aloof and mainly seemed concerned that I would trash the place. I told him of my intentions to restore the building as well as the cemeteries and had earned a friend for life, or death in our case. He was very concerned that the cemeteries needed protection and I couldn't agree more. The previous owner held haunted tours and there was an endless stream of screamers. There were several more ghosts that popped up little by little as word got around that I could see them. So far I counted seven permanent ghosts and several dozen visitors. Julie even came to see my new home. Since marrying her beau she found the nerve to leave the house.

"Please be nice to Skye," I asked her before she faded away. With the place practically surrounded by cemeteries it was no wonder the ghosts found me. Daniel even popped in for a visit and made friends with the ghosts of a little boy and girl who live at the mansion. Luckily the deceased were respectful of my privacy except for one persistent rake.

Tarik kept popping in at the most inopportune moments. Unlike humans vampires domains are free game to other vampires. Whatever makes it impossible to cross uninvited to a human habitat is simply non-existent to vampires. He even showed up on my first night there with Terry. The same night I had decided to take things to a new level, maybe.

"Don't you believe in knocking?" He just barged in while we were watching Underworld Evolutions on my new flat screen. "Sorry to intrude I was just bringing you an urgent assignment."

"Why the personal delivery? Is your internet down?" He didn't even have the good sense to look sorry for interrupting my evening. On the contrary he looked quite smug. "Sorry but this is top priority and we need to discuss this now, alone." Tarik looked pointedly at Terry who was not in the least intimidated.

Terry stretched lazily and gave me a smoldering kiss before leaving us to discuss business. It was a little hard to really enjoy the kiss with Tarik watching but I put on a good show just to spite him. I walked Terry to the door and returned to the living room to confront Tarik. "Never heard of cell phones, doorbells, privacy? You can't just barge in my life all the time. Please respect my space."

It's hard to be mad at someone who looks like your every wet dream come to life. Tarik just stood there patiently listening to me and waiting for my tirade to finish.

He actually looked a little embarrassed and apologized. "I'm truly sorry but this couldn't wait. There has been a kidnapping and I need your help." I looked a question at him without uttering a word.

"Just read the briefing packet and you will understand the urgency." He thrust it into my hand and entered. I read through the folder twice and hated to admit it but he was right, this couldn't wait. A child had been kidnapped and would surely be turned if we didn't act fast and get her back immediately. Valerie was the natural born child of two vampires. The doorbell rang and Tarik let in Viktor and some of the vampires that work with us. I guess I was the last to know.

Viktor kissed me on the cheek and led everyone into the living room.

"Your place is centrally located so we decided to meet here. Well, that and the fact that everyone has been dying to see it. Holy crap! This place is spooky. You got some big balls to try and live here."

The others chimed in. "This is so cool, I wish I had found it." Blake was easygoing and friendly. I had yet to see him ever complain about anything. He wasn't a suck up, at least not figuratively. He was just an agreeable vampire.

"I could never sleep here, it just creeps me out." A female hunter named Leticia shuddered as she looked around. She looks like Barbie but fights like Rambo. A vampire like her is a good surprise when fighting evil kidnappers and pedophiles.

"You would never know what it was just looking at this room. It just looks like a normal living room.." Adam spoke as he walked around looking in doorways and closets. I told them a little bit about the history of the home. "This was originally built as a home, not a mortuary."

The group had entered the neo-classical revival home from the front which had six columns across the length of the building. The entry is grand and the staircase leading up is winding and draped in black tulle and black flowers befitting a mortuary. I hadn't taken them down due to difficulties with one ghost. He's very particular about the decorations..

"The graveyard next door is a nice touch," Tarik added with a wink to me. I knew he was thinking of the night in Odd Fellows when he made love to me, turned me, and then left me. He could have been referring to our most recent incident in Metarie cemetery. I had been helping there with records since their entire history had been ruined during the flooding after Katrina. Either way, his thoughts were definitely lascivious.

"Well, I love this place and it doesn't creep me out at all. The building is marvelous, the architecture solid and I plan to make it a splendid home. I'm turning the upstairs into a studio and the place is big enough to entertain, and I can have offices for Adopt-A-Crypt." I had developed a program to help restore and upkeep tombs in New Orleans and named it Adopt-A-Crypt.

Sasha crossed the room and gracefully draped herself across the couch. Not many people can carry off a leopard print bodysuit. "You have found a treasure indeed, I am jealous." She pouted prettily and Gabe came to placate her by patting her shoulder and murmuring in her ear. I could just imagine the conversation that would follow later. "But darling you must find us a place like this." What Sasha wants, Sasha whines until she gets.

Like a good hostess I offered them some O-positive from the fridge. I certainly wasn't offering the AB negative, which was for special occasions. "Would you like some O-positive? I have Mexican if you like spicy and Italian if you aren't allergic to garlic." Contrary to popular fiction not all vampires are allergic to garlic, I absolutely love it. I passed around bottles of the stuff after a quick warm up.

We began planning for the rescue operation. I couldn't help but think of my own niece as we planned the child's rescue. I knew Valerie's mother vaguely and she was a sweet natured woman. I couldn't imagine what she must be going through.

Viktor had found out where the child was being held. I didn't need to ask how. The people who had her would turn her and use her for child pornography. Valerie was especially valuable because she was a natural vampire. Her parents were already vampires and she was born to them as a vampire. When she dies she will instantly turn no matter what age she is. That makes her especially valuable to the slavers because she is so much stronger than a mortal child. Many of them go insane within a few months of being turned. They become "screamers" and then have to be put down like a horse with a broken leg or something; it's just too cruel to contemplate. This child could last for years, decades, or unthinkably centuries being tortured.

We knew where Valerie was being held and planned to raid the place a few hours before dawn. Viktor knew the area and had actually seen the warehouse when looking for a place for a new club he planned to open. He drew out a map of the building layout and we were each assigned entry points. It was just like a swat operation only with preternatural speed and lots of fangs.

At the predetermined time we each burst in and swarmed the kidnappers. It wasn't that hard. Only a few were vamps, one was a were and the rest were human. I used the compressed holy water on one vampire and he literally went up in flames. The human's made a nice little snack for twenty pissed off vampires. Our vamps were a little pissed that I insisted on snack/rehab instead of draining them dry though. Valerie's parents were there to take care of her and the ending was happy for her after all. Its nights like this that make it all worthwhile. Thwarting the bad guys makes me feel all warm and fuzzy inside, and I got to use my Super-mace. I only wished we had gotten their leader. John was slippery as usual. Viktor's men gathered up some bad guys for questioning.

I returned to my new home on Canal Street and tucked myself in after a warm shower. The "panic" room was now filled with my favorite things. The wrought iron bed from my grandparents place was painted black and draped in black netting and silk. I crawled in with my poofy pillows and snuggled in. I could see all the monitors which showed every room and the entrances. I fell asleep feeling safe and secure.

When I woke I instantly felt something was not right. Someone was in my house. I scanned the monitors and saw nothing out of the ordinary. I slipped on an old robe and went upstairs to check it out. I couldn't figure out what it was. I knew I felt something. I went to the front door and opened it. Tarik was sitting on the steps.

"What are you doing?"

He stood and I took in the work of art that was Tarik. It was way too early to have the brainpower to think right around him.

"I was waiting for you to wake. I want to see the rest of your new home."

This was odd and quite subdued for him but I let it slide.

"Come inside. Just give me a minute though." I ran back downstairs and brushed my teeth and hair. It's just not fair for him to show up looking so good and I look like death warmed over. That is so like him. I was mumbling and grumbling to myself when he came up behind me.

I had just begun to change from my sweatpants and t-shirt. I was standing there in my underwear when he slid his arms around my waist. Good grief I did not have the will power for this. It had been so long since he had held me. It was like coming home, feeling at peace, secure. All of the issues we had were burning in the back of my mind but my body needed him and shoved those issues aside. I turned in his arms and sank my teeth into his neck, licking and sucking, just a little taste. Just the tiniest taste of him brings me completely over the edge. He cupped my ass and I wrapped my legs around him.

We kissed like starving people afraid we would never feed again. I peeled his shirt off and it hung down his back exposing his alabaster skin. Tarik walked us to the bed and put me down. I released him from his jeans and they slid to the floor followed by his shirt. "You know this doesn't change anything?" I asked as he leaned in to kiss me. He looked pained and told me, "I just need you, no strings." He looked vulnerable but I know everything he does is calculated. I knew his words were a lie. Tarik came here planning this no doubt. I wasn't arguing though I couldn't get him out of my mind. He helped me with that problem and we began to reacquaint ourselves. I traced the angles of his torso with my tongue, slowly tasting every inch that I had denied myself so long.

His long hair spilled out like ink that outshone the satin sheets. It was like catnip for me, I just wanted to roll in it. Nothing marred his alabaster skin. I breathed in the scent of him as I buried my nose in all that hair.

All too soon my bliss was ended with just a few words.

"I want you to quit working with the council." I thought, here we go again. He wants me to be this sweet little innocent he thought he knew.

"You know I can't do that. We've had this discussion before. I do this because I want to. Every creep I rid the world of makes one more child safe. It's just like the cemeteries, I am helping them because they need help and I have the ability to help."

"You're not the only one who is working on this though and it's very dangerous. I just don't want anything to happen to you."

I could see the genuine concern in his eyes but it still didn't change my mind.

"I have to do this. I can't be with you if you keep trying to push me around. Just go! It's what you're good at."

I went in the bathroom and sobbed when I heard his footsteps fading. Now he does what I say. That just figures doesn't it?

Chapter 31

I didn't see or hear from Tarik again and with all the preparations for my sister's visit and the Mardi Gras madness going on I had kept him out of my mind. I had a couple of jobs for the council to get out of the way and I concentrated on that for the time being.

We found a mole in the council. No doubt Joshua was a little weasel before he died. Now he's a rat, just not the head rat. That was who I was gunning for. The trouble was that we don't know who he is. All we know is that he is a mega computer geek and has more money than Bill Gates. I had been holding off on killing Joshua in hopes that he would lead me to his boss. The hard part was convincing Joshua that I was for sale to the highest bidder. He knew me and knew what I did.

We met at Shanahan's Pub and huddled in a corner to talk.

"I was under the impression that you hated his kind."

I gave him a deadpan stare and finally spoke. "I don't discriminate; I hate everyone, its money that I love. That and the freedom it buys me. Just so you know; I don't want to meet your boss, I want his job. Go tell him that I'm his only supplier from now on. If he wants merchandise he gets it from me. If he tries anything else I will personally kill every client he ever dreamed of having."

"How are you gonna back that up?"

"Ask your boss how business has been since I moved to town." I knew it had to have gone down at least seventy percent, maybe even eighty. It was a gamble but I knew there was no way I would get near him any other way. I can get you another true blood vampire child but it'll cost you one million."

He spit out his beer and just laughed. "You're crazy."

"No, I'm not crazy. I am just a business woman with the ability to acquire that which is coveted by your boss. Just give him the message and tell him I need an answer by tomorrow night."

I left Joshua there and hoped he would take the bait. Two things could happen. One, he would fall for it and I would get a chance to meet the boss. The other was that he wouldn't believe me and he would try to kill me personally or via the thugs he tended to hire. Either way I get to find out who he is and with a little luck I get to kill him.

After I left the bar I headed to Club Morte to tell Viktor what I had done. I knew he would be furious but it was time we dealt with this guy and no one else seemed to be doing the job. The bouncer was a werewolf named Todd who always seemed to be on duty. He was big and strong and meaner than the devil. No one got past him unless he wanted them to. I waved to him as I skipped past the line and through the doors. He looked like he was about to rip a new one for some underage guys trying to get in.

Leslie Brown

Viktor was behind the bar restocking. Business was always good but it is very hard to keep good help and Mardi Gras season is the busiest of the year.

"Hey, it's good to see you doing some manual labor. I'm impressed."

He finished filling the boxes with empty bottles and stacked them at the end of the counter. After Viktor finished he came around and placed an arm around my shoulders to whisper in my ear.

"I hope you are here for pleasure not business. I've been missing you terribly."

I had forced things to cool off but that didn't stop him from trying every chance he got. His deep sexy voice traveled down my neck like warm molasses. If it didn't complicate things so much between the three of us, Tarik being the third I would succumb. He kissed my neck softly and that made things way down low quiver and purr. If I didn't stop this now I never would.

"I had a meeting with Joshua." My words had an immediate effect, sort of like a kick in the nuts. He pulled back and groaned.

"Say you're kidding. Surely you know how dangerous he can be. That little weasel has been a thorn in my side for years." We only just learned the extent of his treachery. The only reason he is still alive is because we haven't decided just how much to make him suffer first.

"I'm not kidding." I hopped off the barstool and began walking towards the office and Viktor followed. We entered and he shut the door to drown out the music so that we could talk.

"I told him that I want to meet his boss." I waited to see his reaction and he just kept getting madder. I hoped he wouldn't blow up. I need him to be on my side and help me set up a trap.

"I told Joshua that I was taking over as a supplier and that if they didn't use me they would be cut down."

"And you really think he bought that? He's probably just placating you to set up a trap himself."

"Of course he is. He'd be stupid not to try it. He understands that I am the reason his business is almost nonexistent lately."

Deja Voodoo   116

"Sure you are, but was it wise to point that out? He'll be determined to take you out now. That was so stupid!" He paced and raged at me but I could see his mind was thinking about the possibilities.

"I also told him I could get a true born vampire child." Viktor stopped in his tracks and turned to face me. An evil grin spread across his face.

"That's it! He won't be able to resist. We just need to figure out a plan to make this work and keep you alive. He grabbed me in a hug and kissed the top of my head. "I'll help you."

We worked together and came up with some ideas. A girl who works at the club is a Vamphaerie. Most people mistook her for a dwarf and she let them think so to cover her hide. We called her in and she agreed to help us. Heather would pose as the vampire child. She is small and has a childlike quality that with a little dress up will work perfectly as long as she kept her wings hidden. Vamphaeries are particularly tough and I was sure she could hold her own with anyone.

My cell phone rang and it was Joshua. I wiggled my eyebrows to let Viktor know it was him. After I hung up I told Viktor what the plan was. "He said to meet him tomorrow night." Joshua had given me an address in the warehouse district and told me to bring the child.

"I heard every word." I kept forgetting how good vampire hearing was. Of course he heard everything. We Googled the address and went there to check out the place and finish our plans. We were keeping this low key and only bringing a couple of new vampires as backup. They would pose as my bodyguard and Joshua didn't know them.

Tarik had left town after our last failure at a relationship and that was fine by me. He probably wouldn't have gone along with it anyway. Viktor asked Todd the werewolf to help also and when everything was set, I started to leave. Viktor stopped me and asked me to stay with him.

"I'm not trying to push you, I just don't want to take any chances right now. Stay with me just for tonight. I promise I will try and take advantage." He grinned up at me and his pierced eyebrow twinkled like his mischievous eyes. He was probably right; it would be just like Joshua to try something sneaky tonight. I agreed but told him we were sleeping in separate beds.

"No sneaky stuff."

We left the club for his home in the Garden District. I followed Viktor to his safe room and told him that since there was only one bed he would just have to control himself. I slipped out of my boots and jeans and crawled in under the covers in my t-shirt. Viktor took his time undressing in order to give me a full show. I considered hiding under the cover but why waste a good show. He was quite stunning with all the body art and sinewy muscles. Considering we only had a few minutes until sunrise I was reasonably safe. When Viktor slid in beside me I reached out to hold him while I slept. My last thought was that it was nice to have someone to hold. I had never spent the night with a man before. Seconds later dawn pulled me under.

Chapter 32

I woke still holding him in exactly the same way. That was one strange feeling. You lie down and sleep but you never dream, no tossing, or turning. I know that I am technically dead but the only time I feel like it is when I wake in the evening.

Victor woke just as I did and I smiled at him. I knew that he was at my mercy. He hadn't fed and it was my turn to tease him. I rose and stretched lazily, peeling off my t-shirt slowly. Then I bent to remove my underwear and tossed them at him as I headed for the door and pressed the locking mechanism to release us. I went to the master bedroom to enjoy the shower there. It was one of those totally decadent ones with spray heads everywhere. A girl could just die for a shower like that. I really need to put one in my house now that I have room to do such renovation.

I shampooed and used the masculine smelling body wash that Viktor always used. I was just rinsing the conditioner off my hair when he joined me. He began to lather that devilish body and all I could think of was how I wished I was the soap. I imagined rubbing myself all over him the way the suds trailed over every curve and bulge.

Bulge! Shit, that meant he had fed. "You don't play fair. I thought you refused to imbibe in the bottled stuff?"

"Yes, but I'm so glad I stocked some for emergencies."

I devoured him with my eyes and struggled with my conscience. It had been less than a week since I had almost been with not only Terry; but also Tarik. Did this classify me as a slut? It's not like I had to worry about disease or pregnancy. We don't get diseases and the chances of pregnancy are a billion to one. It did seem a little slutty to me but he looked so good and I had been so deprived as a human. Vampires don't think about sex the way humans do but I still had some human feelings and it was hard to be so casual.

The water played off his muscles and when he began to lather himself down there I totally lost it. Damn he was just too much, literally. Is it gauche to drool? The shower would probably hide it anyway. My inner argument raged on and finally he made the decision for me.

"I don't want to pick out matching Beemers, I just want to fuck you." He reached for me and filled my mouth with kisses so finely honed they rendered my senseless. I let myself go and began to enjoy what he offered. My fingers played over his body as I slid down to take him in my mouth. I needed to taste him, to feel the silken shaft gliding in and out of me. I drew away and licked the base searching for the right spot and then bit down letting my fangs pierce him. I drank and savored the musky flavor of his blood. I gave the wound one last lap of the tongue and stared him in the eye.

I liked the taste of him in my mouth. I loved the feel of him beneath my teeth. I crave the feeling of him doing the same. Pleasure mixed with pain bringing me over the edge. He lifted me to stand on the edge of the built in bench as he returned the favor, pulling the blood from me as I screamed above him. The orgasm was fast and furious making me shudder into his mouth. He rose and I wrapped myself around his body and slid down to impale myself on him. He turned and braced me against the wall of the shower and the warm water slid over me once again. Viktor bent his head to suck and pierce one nipple to drink again as he slid in and out of me. The shower made the fit even tighter as it washed away the natural lubricant which brought me just to the edge of pain once again. My brain said; if he stops I will kill him.

He pulled out and I whimpered at the loss but soon realized he was just moving us. With me still wrapped around him he walked into the bedroom and began where he left off. With his tongue he traced every inch of my body. I bit and licked at any part I could reach, ravenous for him. Viktor rolled me over and entered which made me feel every inch of him. We set a frantic pace and finally finished together completely worn out but quite a bit less stressed.

Viktor is the quintessential bad boy that every girl needs to wrap herself around at least once in her life. We had been quite acrobatic but being vampires we heal fast. "I hope that within a few minutes I will actually be able to walk." I laughed as he said that. "Oh, did the big bad vampire hurt himself?" We teased each other and finally I got up to look for clothes. I had some things there in case I needed a quick change after a job so I put on a clean pair of undies, jeans, and a t-shirt after another quick shower, alone. My boots were downstairs in the safe room and Viktor retrieved them for me while I was in the shower and left them by my pile of clothes. While I dressed he showered. I heard him from the bedroom, "sure you don't want to join me again?" "That's okay honey; just a little bit of you is enough to go a long way. Just get finished, we need to go."

When we were both ready we left his Garden District home to meet the others at Club Morte. The Warehouse District is not far and as we passed the lovely homes, shops, and businesses carved out of the "American" part of the city I admired the view. My eye slid over to Viktor and stayed a bit too long ogling him. He turned and grinned at me. What an ego, the man was puffed up like a crooked politician with a pocket full of bribe money. "Don't even think about it. We are not going to make a habit of this." He pulled up to a light to stop and drawled, "I don't know how you're gonna' possibly resist." I snorted, "Spare me." The light turned green and we crossed busy Magazine street with its' many shops and café's.

Chapter 33

We arrived at C

lub Morte to find that Heather had outdone herself. If I hadn't known her I would have thought she was a nine year old child. She and my two body guards rode with me in Viktor's SUV. Viktor followed with the bouncer and another vampire. Two more werewolves had gone ahead to be in place early. I circled the building twice and parked the car across the street. We crossed and knocked on the door marked 6235. For a while I thought they had been screwing with me and didn't plan to show but the door finally opened. Joshua stood there with a vampire I didn't know.

I did know that he wasn't who I sought. This vampire was way too new.

The four of us entered the building and submitted to a frisking for weapons and wires. They even checked Heather who pretended to be scared. It turned out that she was quite the little actress. Then they led us into the warehouse where four more men waited. It was dark and even with vampire sight it was hard to make out the features of one man. He wore a hat pulled down low and his collar hid even more. I figured that must be him so I confronted him boldly.

"Do you have my money?"

He nodded to one of the other three and that man brought a bag out. He removed a computer and opened it to show the account with one million dollars waiting to be transferred to my account.

"May I see the girl?" He spoke with a raspy voice which sounded familiar. I moved closer and answered. "I don't like working with someone I don't know.

"Show me the girl!" He screamed at me.

I nodded to my guards and they brought her to him. He bent and looked at Heather, turning her chin left and then right. Her lips quivered and tears slid down her cheeks. He reached down and grabbed her so fast it was a blur. One second he was bent over her and the next instant she was tossed thirty feet into the wall.

"Did you think I would fall for this trap?" He was still hidden from view and everything went to hell fast. Heather shook herself off and flew at him with her fangs barred. Two of his thugs stopped her and she fought like a little banshee. My guards rushed to help and were attacked by Joshua and the other vampire. I went to help Heather and the bastard tried to get away.

He was met at the door by two fully transformed werewolves. I had never seen someone that I knew and had changed and I stared for a minute before continuing. Viktor rushed in to join the melee and we rescued Heather by each attacking a vampire. I ripped into the neck of the one I had and he latched onto my arm like a pitbull. I tore back and pulled out muscle and skin which rendered him temporarily out of commission. This outfit was definitely ruined. Even as I dug in my back pocket for the silver zip ties my arm began to heal. I hog tied the vampire and handed another set to Viktor to do the same.

One on one a vampire had a chance with a werewolf but two to one was a no brainer. They drug one vampire back in and literally devoured him. I can't say that I felt sorry for him. I might have given him a less messy option though. In the end we had three vampires tied and the leader still managed to get away. We cleaned up the mess in the warehouse and took the prisoners back to the club through the back entrance that led into the office.

We had two choices. We could either just kill the vampires or Viktor could blood oath them to him. He wouldn't do that lightly and we locked them up in some holding cells built to withstand any preternatural creature. Viktor would do some investigating and determine if the three were worth saving.

I left through the back and went home to shower and sleep in my own house. This had been the longest night and I needed to sleep and finish healing completely. I pulled an old blanket from the back of the Jeep and spread it out on the Neoprene seats. They were water repellant but blood was another issue. I pulled into the back of the former mortuary which I now called home and let myself in.

My home is not what everyone would want but it suits me perfectly. I showered and by the time I was dried off the wound on my arm had healed. Hooray for vamp healing! I went to the kitchen and got a couple of bottles of O-positive-Italian and downed them with a slice of cold pizza. There's nothing better than pizza. I curled up on the couch to watch HGTV on the big screen and just vegged out for a while to relax before dawn. One of the ghosts, a woman in her forties named Lauren came in and sat with me. She doesn't talk but she is companionable.

The other ghosts milled around me doing what they normally do. They had become comfortable with me here and it was like coming home to a busy family. The caretaker who used to work in the building busied himself cleaning and adjusting things to his rigid preference. Some things he would allow and others he was adamant that they be kept in the exact spot he had chosen. When I tried to take down the black mourning

Leslie Brown   123

decorations on the banister in the entrance stairway he actually slapped my hand once. The two children, a boy and a girl played hide and seek. If you could ignore the fact that we were all dead we were a happy family.

Chapter 34

Months ago I drew a design for the Krewe du Morte for Viktor. The vampire council sponsored a float for the Mardi Gras Parades. The people at Blaine Kern's Mardi Gras World were building the million dollar float which would hold 50 riders. I took the streetcar on Canal to the ferry and went over the river to see the finished design. Over the river, my reputation now kept me safe in their territory.

The fiber optic filled float was designed around the Scary side of New Orleans. Topping the massive structure was a crypt with a ghoul crawling out on top. The facades of several more

Deja Voodoo

crypts flanked either side and continued along to the back. The crypts were surrounded by a myriad of vampires, ghosts, pirates, Voodoo Loa's, and the loup gareau; the Cajun version of the werewolf. The front of the float had six black horses from hell pulling a hearse.

The finished float far exceeded my expectations it was so beautiful. I couldn't wait to ride on it and throw the plastic doubloons I had also designed. Each Krewe member would throw thousands of the doubloons, beads, and plastic cups in a single parade. With only three weeks left before the uptown parade all the riders were scrambling with last minute costume preparations.

Mardi Gras World's warehouses were bursting with finished floats. As I walked through I saw some of my favorites like Endymion and Bacchus. The Endymion float with the beautiful river nymph was one of the longest at 150 feet long and carries 200 passengers. That portion is a steamboat and is only part of the entire group of five floats that make up the super Krewe of Endymion. Each Krewe has a theme and this year the theme for Krewe Morte is resurrection.

The artists on staff here took my drawings and brought them to life using Styrofoam, wire, metal, wood, and paper mache'. First the base was created from an old unused float. Often they reuse floats and characters just changing them and adding more. The tombs were created with plywood and the curvilinear forms added with Styrofoam. The creatures were made by gluing huge blocks of Styrofoam together and then carving the details and also paper mache'd. The detailed pieces are painted with a primer and then airbrushed to get the beautiful color. Millions of LED lights are added to create a flowing glow. I came in periodically to oversee the project and even got to work on some of the sculptures myself. The artists who work on the floats have a very enviable job. Some of them have families who have done this for generations. Besides Mardi Gras floats the company also creates things for businesses like Disney and for Hollywood.

After taking the ferry back across to New Orleans I checked in on the galleries and then left to return home. I got off the streetcar by the mortuary but instead of going inside I walked up the street to Oddfellows. The cemetery was quiet and for once I

Leslie Brown

wasn't bombarded with a hundred requests. As that odd luxury sank into my brain I realized that something was not right. It was too quiet. I went over to Daniel's tomb and whispered his name. He stuck his head out of the front of the granite slab that had replaced the old broken one. It was weird seeing his head like a mounted deer head on a wall.

"What's up? Why is it so quiet around here? Daniel looked left and right before speaking in a whisper. "There was a Hoodoo man here and he was up to no good." A Hoodoo is another version of Voodoo from what I had learned while looking for an end to the curse.

"He was messing around on the back wall where that cast iron sarcophagus is. You know the one that is screwed shut?" I knew the one he talked about and had often wondered about it. The cemetery was in very bad shape for years and the sarcophagus lay on the bottom row of wall tombs sticking out a little bit. There was no faceplate to identify who was in it and whoever it was they weren't sociable or they had passed into the light. I always thought it was kind of creepy with the many bolts that screwed the two ornate pieces of the metal coffin together. Who needs a coffin made of cast iron anyway?

The sarcophagus was small and very old, probably for a woman judging from the size and design. I told Daniel to go to sleep and I left him to go investigate. The restorers had put the sarcophagus back in and put a new faceplate labeled unknown to cover the tomb. On the grass below it there was a candle that had burnt down to a nub and beside it was a little doll. The doll was not as crude as most Voodoo dolls but very realistic. The doll had long blonde hair, red lipstick, and wore a pink dress with a bow at the waist. It was surrounded by flower petals and candy with bright wrappers. There were black X's drawn on the faceplate and it reeked of rum. The entire thing gave me the creeps.

I backed away from the scene and saw a ghost watching me. He was a young man of eighteen years wearing a civil war uniform. He had died in the battle of Shiloh and resided in the cast Iron tomb near the sarcophagus. He never spoke but his expression said enough. He shook his head and disappeared into

Deja Voodoo

his crypt. This was not good. What on earth was going on here? I would have to get Jo down here to check this out. I left the quiet cemetery and headed home.

The next night after I rose I went to Voodoo Joe's to see Jo and tell her about the strange happenings at Oddfellows Rest Cemetery. She was behind the counter with a lady who could be anyone's grandma. It never ceases to amaze me who I see in places like this. They finished their transaction and Jo pulled out a package and laid it on the counter for me. Someone left this for you. I wasn't expecting anything but I took what felt like a book and slid it into my backpack. I told her about what I had seen at the cemetery and she seemed very troubled about it but assured me that she would go over and check it out. I left it in her hands and went to finish making my Mardi Gras plans.

I had groceries delivered for Stacia who was walking and talking now. The fridge was stocked with everything from ordinary American to Transylvanian AB negative which was the most expensive of bloods. They would be here in a few days and and would stay for the month before mardi gras. I had been furnishing the bedrooms for Stacia and her nanny, painting murals on the walls for her and decorated with a Mardi Gras kids theme. While my sister and her husband slept they needed someone to watch over Stacia so she had a nanny. I planned to sleep at the gallery and let Alex and Luke have my safe room. The nanny would watch Stacia as they slept and she could use one of the guest bedrooms which had not been sun-proofed yet. "It must be frustrating to be helpless every evening when your child might need you." I muttered while working on the room. The ghosts watching mumbled in unison, "very," "ain't it so."

For Stacia's safety while here I added more security and beefed up the windows with bulletproof glass. I hired a werewolf to keep watch during the day as well. Who me, paranoid? Hell yes when it came to them. I could deal with the everyday insanity but they were on vacation they don't need any Dracu-drama. Alex wanted to meet up with some local Wiccans and stock up at the Herb Import Company across the street. She was still into the holistic medicine thing and helped many people in her town that didn't trust traditional medicine or just preferred the natural approach.

I loaded up the Jeep with a few new paintings to take to the gallery and headed out. Parking is always a pain in the butt in the French Quarter. It took forever to find a spot and when I finally did it was pretty far away. Being a vampire made me very strong but someone would notice if I carried 300 pounds in canvas and frames in one trip. I took a couple of pieces and headed to Royal Street.

It was after hours and I had to disable the alarm and let myself in. I tried to be quiet but Skye woke and came to see what I had brought. My recent work included some parade paintings and they were different. Each one featured a float with people throwing beads and in the foreground masked revelers caught them. The frames were heavy and made with beads and doubloons incorporated with other found objects.

"These are too cool! I think I like them even better than the others." Sky walked to the Jeep with me and we retrieved the others. Naturally when we got back to the shop there was a parking space available right out front. "That's why I hardly ever drive. Hopefully the flying thing will kick in soon, how cool will that be?" Skye remarked as we let ourselves back inside the gallery.

We took the last of the paintings inside and set them up. Skye took a painting out of the window and replaced it with one of the new ones. She had been making masks and couldn't work fast enough for the buyers. There were a few of them interspersed among her other sculptures.

The other side of the gallery housed the more sedate portraits. They were more somber and haunting. The sexy vampires and lycanthropes portrayed were all the rage now. Everyone wanted to be painted and I was becoming more discriminating in my acceptance of commissions. I had just finished Mrs. John Blake's portrait who is the mayor's wife last month and hadn't accepted any new commissions yet..

Skye came in and saw me looking at a portrait of Viktor. I was thinking of the night we had shared.

"You did it again, didn't you?" She slapped me on the shoulder and laughed at my misery.

"Why can't I keep my fangs off that guy?"

"Maybe because he's the hottest thing on two feet? Why do you even try to resist? You know the old saying? I wouldn't throw him out of bed unless he wanted to fuck on the floor."

"With him its, floor, shower, ceiling, hearse...hey! We actually did it in a bed this time. You would have been so proud."

"Quit stressing out over it. You have no ties to anyone, just enjoy yourself. I can't believe you stayed a virgin so long. You've got some kind of will power. Now that you can have sex you need to just let it flow. If I had an hour with him and a roll of Duct Tape I could die a happy girl."

"You're so bad! Why should I take advice from a nympho like you?"

"I know what I want and I'm not afraid to take it." That sounded just like Viktor. I swear they are twins sometimes.

"I can't help but feel weird about sleeping with two guys within the same week."

"What! Who else did you do? Who else was there?"

I winced and silently berated myself for letting that slip. Oh, well she might as well know. "It was Tarik. But we didn't actually seal the deal. And I planned to go to the next level with Terry but Tarik tripped that up. Maybe it's for the best. My life is complicated enough"

"Yes! Oh my God! Tell me every single detail."

I told her enough and saying some of it out loud made it sound more rational in my own mind. Viktor was irresistible, even if I get my shit together with Tarik can I ever say no to him? Tarik was different. My need for him was soul deep. When he's not around it's like I forget to breathe and then when he's there I can't breathe deeply enough.

I didn't know where I stood with Tarik but I know that I have much to explore with Viktor. I left feeling as little better and went straight to Viktor's house. When I make a decision it's instant action. I let myself in and he was watching music videos in his home theatre. I went straight to him and straddled his legs in the huge recliner. My hands drew him close and I kissed him with renewed determination. I never had to worry with Viktor; he was always there for me and wasn't offended when I made him back off. He really was just right for what I needed now.

Leslie Brown

He pulled the top over my head and bared my breasts to the night. We came together that night and many more to follow. Once I quit fighting the attraction and instead embraced it. I began to feel secure in my future. The only thing that remained in question was Tarik but I was beginning to get used to that. Patience is on the side of the vampire that embraces it. I was patient if nothing else. I knew that one day things would be right with Tarik. It's like eating a bowl of sherbet but knowing that someday you can have a dark chocolate cappuccino swirl triple dip cone.

Chapter 35

Alex, Luke, Stacia and the nanny arrived on a Thursday at three a.m. They had been driving for hours and everyone was exhausted so I quickly showed Stacia and the nanny, Maria to their rooms. I had painted Stacia's walls with murals of Mardi Gras including unicorns leading a float. Unicorns are her favorite animal. The toddler bed was hand carved and looked like a coach that Cinderella might ride in. The scenes on the walls had a parade of mystical creatures travelling down Canal Street. I filled the room with toys and stuffed animals. When she saw all the toys she got her second wind and began to play with everything. I left her with Maria and showed Alex and Luke the safe room.

"This place is amazing," Alex said as she ran her hand up the banister. "Did you tell the ghosts we would be here? I don't want to spook them or vice versa." Alex was trying to open her mind to see the ghosts but having trouble. She was also afraid that Stacia might get scared if she saw one. We passed the back hallway and took the stairs down to the lower floor, the old embalming area. We passed a window looking out onto the cemetery next door and Luke remarked, "doesn't this creep you out?" He visibly shivered and I chuckled at his squeamish nature. "You are so dead meat." I teased. "The iddy biddy vampire is afwaid" I teased him. Alex joined in and he finally left us to see how Stacia was doing.

"We are so bad, but that is so much fun." We fell into fits of giggling as we finished touring the house. When we got upstairs to the gallery and opened the door a ghost popped out, scaring us. "What the hell!" Alex screamed and I jumped three feet. "How do you like being scared. I'm sick of being stereotyped, so lay off.' One of the ghosts, an old man who just grumbles said before vanishing. I stuck my tongue out at him and he hollered. "I saw that!" He was an old undertaker that worked here and he was very picky about everything in the place. I told Alex about him and warned her. "Don't even try to remove the black tulle from the banisters. He's libel to strangle you with it. Some things here you just can't mess with. If I redecorate and he doesn't like it the changes are reversed immediately. I moved that coffin in the drawing room I don't know how many times. Now I just leave it alone. It makes a good place to put blankets though.

We went back upstairs and saw Maria unpacking in her room and across the hall Stacia was busy playing with all the new toys. The two child ghosts who live in the house were with her playing and chatting away like they were best friends. They didn't talk to me much, maybe they were afraid because I am a vampire. I heard them tell Stacia their names, Matthew and Lizzy. I hadn't even gotten that info out of them yet. Daniel comes over from the cemetery and plays with them but to my knowledge they hadn't offered much information yet let alone their names. I was curious as to whether they had lived in this building while it was a home or had just adopted the place. Apparently the ghosts didn't scare

Stacia or she didn't know they were ghosts. We came into the room and the children looked up. Stacia ran to me and hugged me tight.

"Aunt Kat! I love these toys. Tank you berry much." I hugged her back and lifted her high in the air bringing a squeal of delight from the tiny child. "You're very welcome. Do you like the paintings?" She nodded in assent and struggled to get down in order to play with her new friends. Stacia looked up and said, "When I go home please let the ghosts stay in my room and they can play with my toys. It's nice to share." I smiled and assured them all that they could play with the toys and stay any time they wished. Matthey smiled shyly at me and Lizzy came up to give me a hug. It was the first positive contact I had seen out of them. We left them to play together.

"I guess that answers our question, Stacia can see the ghosts." Alex noted as we walked down the stairs to the main floor. "Often children are more open to spirits. Have you ever wondered when a dog stared at something you couldn't see? Alex nodded. "I always heard that kids and animals are sensitive, now I believe it." I left via the front door as we descended the steps, hugging my sis goodbye. "Call me if you need anything. I nodded to the were guard as I headed down the steps to the street.

That night I slept at Victor's place. I had originally planned to stay at the gallery but that was before. Now we were spending most nights together. We had to expand that whole ceiling, floor, shower, hearse, repertoire. So far we added an elevator, the ferry, the parade float, and a coffee shop, and a street car to name a few. At sunset I left for home and he went to Club Morte.

Alex and Luke were up with Stacia who also kept evening hours. She was slurping up Fruit Loops and giggling at the faces her daddy made as he fed her. We talked and I explained the plan for the parades and activities we would attend. We had a snack from my bottled supply and then set out to find a real meal. Maria stayed with Stacia and the guards were on duty front and back.

The streetcars run in front of the house and we took one to the French Quarter. I showed them some places where there are willing donors and we walked the crowded streets. During the

Deja Voodoo

weeks of Mardi Gras there were thousands of people there every night in the Quarter. I took the time to search out the perfect snack. As I passed people I could read their minds to find a target. Their thoughts jumbled together.

"I've gotta piss, Look at those tits, I drank too much, need more beer." I found one that had some not so nice thoughts about how his wife would never know he had just left a prostitute. "Bingo!" I veered away from Alex and Luke and followed the guy into a bar. I squeezed in next to him at the counter and let him get just the wrong idea. Ten minutes later he was a quart low and wondering if there was an all night flower shop open because he had an urge to buy flowers for his wife.

I met back up with Luke and Alex who had also fed and we left the Bourbon Street crowd for Club Morte. I was losing my aversion to dresses as I learned how useful they could be in the right situation. Tonight I wore a black long sleeved dress with a full skirt that hit mid thigh. The back was scooped low and had a chain at the neck to keep it from falling off. I wore thigh high boots with a two inch heel. My hair was loose and the copper curls danced down my back.

Alex approved and had told me so before we left the house. I hadn't told her about Viktor and when we arrived at the club we were greeted at the door by him. Well, mostly the greeting was for me. He took one look at my outfit and growled low in his throat before pulling me close to kiss him. The look in his eyes made me loose all brain function and I was startled by Alex when she touched my elbow.

"Hello, earth to Katrina? Is there something you need to tell me?" I broke the gaze between us and looked at my sister. The look she gave me was full of promise. I was really going to get it when we were alone. We normally don't keep secrets but everything was happening so fast I just hadn't told her. She knew about the first time in the hearse but that was it.

"Hello Alex, Luke, and welcome to my club, it's good to see you again." Viktor shook Luke's hand and kissed Alex on the cheek. We are twins but I favored our mother and she looks like our father. Viktor led us inside and we settled at his private table. Tonight Dilana was headlining. I heard that she was coming and I made sure Viktor saved us a spot. The table was raised and to the right side of the stage so the view was perfect. Viktor knows she is my favorite singer and probably booked her just for that reason. Now a band from Lafayette called 7th Summer was playing. They had been here before and I was really getting in to their music.

Luke really seemed to like them too. We listened for a while and Alex asked me to go to the ladies room with her. I knew what was coming because being vampires we didn't need to go to the restroom. We couldn't even see ourselves in the mirrors even if they had any in there. Instead I took her to the office and gave her a chance to berate me for not telling her about Viktor.

"Since when have you two been a couple? I can't believe you didn't tell me about this." She held up her hand to keep me from answering and continued. "I guess you didn't have time to mention it. I thought you were seeing Terry. What happened to him? Don't you know that you're only going to cause more trouble between you and Tarik, not to mention him and Viktor? What else haven't you told me".

She ran out of breath so I began explaining. "A while back Tarik and I almost shared a night together. I thought we would finally straighten things out but I was wrong. He wants me to quit working, and I don't mean the art gallery. Some other stuff happened and I figured out that Viktor is who I want to be with right now. I broke the news to Terry and he was okay with it. We had some sparks but they just weren't that bright anyway."

"I hope you know what you're doing. This could come back to bite you in the ass you know."

"I'm done with worrying about Tarik. From now on I am going to live for myself. For now that includes Viktor. I don't know what will happen in the future but who does?"

The door opened and Viktor stepped in. "I hope I'm not intruding. Luke wants to dance and he's not my type." Alex left us to go dance with Luke.

"Luke told me that they didn't know about us. How'd she take it?"

"She's just concerned, that's all."

"You're not sorry about this are you?"

"What could you possibly be referring too?" I batted my eyelashes at him and pulled him close. He backed me up against the desk and showed me exactly what he meant. He may not be Mr. Right but he was definitely Mr. Right now.

We made it back out just in time to see Dilana's entrance. She did the cool Voodoo song and on the encore sang Supersoul. This was the first time Alex and Luke had seen her live and they were blown away. The two of them left the club to explore on their own and I stayed with Viktor. When they left I asked Viktor about the three vampires we had taken prisoner.

"What have you decided about our unwelcome guests?

He shook his head and told me what he found out about them. "Michael might be worth saving but two of them are probably lost causes. Michael is from Philadelphia and has a reputation as muscle for hire. He says he didn't know what they wanted the kid for and word is he wouldn't do that type of work if he knew. The other two knew what they were up to. One is a perv himself and is definitely on my shitlist. The other will do anything for money. All three are rogues." Many rogue vampires have no ties and end up being the ones that endanger us all with their activities. "I can't find any ties to any master vampire in the United States."

"It sounds like they both need to be put out of our misery. Have you asked the first guy about blood oathing to you?"

Yes, but I wanted to get your take on it. Do you want to go down and talk to him? I really would like to get you're opinion." Did I hear right? Was a guy actually asking my opinion? Pinch me please.

I went up on tiptoes and kissed him softly on the cheek and smiled. "Thanks."

"For what?"

"You actually care about my opinion." I saw him shrug it off but I could tell he was pleased with himself. "It's not every master vampire that will actually deign to ask the opinion of a newbie like me." Sometimes it's rotten being a young vampire. It's like being at the kid table at Thanksgiving even when you're over eighteen.

We left the office through the side entrance and went down the stairs to the holding cells. They were made to withstand vampires, lycanthropes, and zombies, ghouls, you name it. Sometimes a zombie is raised and left on its own and becomes a revenant, mindless eater. When that happens they are almost impossible to keep under control. The ones that are loose around here get picked up and brought to Club Morte. As soon as possible the problem ones are laid to rest.

Right now the three detainees were waiting their fate and it looked like I get to help decide. Oh goody. We walked by the cells one by one and Viktor told me about each detainee. When we got to the one that he wanted me to speak to I looked at Michael through the glass. I barely remembered what he looked like. Now I looked a little closer. Michael was not what a gun for hire might look like. He looked like a pirate or surfer with his long blonde hair, lean body, and he actually had a tan. It must be a spray on.

Michael looked a little pissed but was obviously trying to control it. Under the circumstances he was holding it together quite well. Emotions played across his face as we watched, he must have sensed we were there. Viktor pushed the button on the wall that allowed the prisoner to hear us. "I'm bringing someone in. Will you behave yourself?" The vampire nodded and Viktor motioned for the guards to open up. He walked in first and I followed. There was a table and chairs in the center of the room. The vampire sat at the table, hands and feet shackled with silver cuffs and chains.

We joined him at the table and I spoke first. "Why should we let you live?" He looked straight at me and said: "You shouldn't." That was not what I expected at all and I questioned him further. "Did you know you were helping a child predator?"

He shifted uncomfortably and shook his head. "No, never! I would have killed him myself if I had known what John was up to. A friend gave him my name and I was told it was a custody battle. As I said if I had known I would have taken him out myself. I don't work for freaks." He growled the last and struggled to control his anger.

"If we let you live you will have to blood oath to Viktor or another master vampire. We can't let you be a rogue anymore.

Obviously you can't make decisions on your own, but it's your decision."

He hung his head and seemed to be warring with himself over the decision. Suddenly he looked up at me through his tangled hair and spoke softly. "If I have to be blood oathed I want it to be you."

I was stunned. "I'm not a master vampire. I'm only a couple of years old. You must be mistaken."

Viktor started laughing and I glared at him. "It's not funny. I can't be responsible for him. I can barely take care of myself." I crossed my arms and glared back at them both. It wasn't like we were talking about adopting a puppy. He was a full blown killer.

Michael spoke to me and his beautiful blue eyes were hard to ignore. "When you came into the warehouse I recognized you. I have been hearing things about your work, quick, clean. You've almost single handedly cleaned this city of predators. If that's not a master vampire I don't know what is. You see what needs to be done and you do it."

"Viktor, talk some sense into this guy." I looked at Viktor for support and was surprised to hear that he had actually thought about this as well. "Michael is not entirely wrong. You have the power of a master vampire." I glared at him, not sure if I should feel complimented or pissed.

Michael watched us and added his opinion. "She smells like a master vampire, and like you"

"What the hell is that supposed to mean? I smell like a master vampire?" Then I turned on Viktor. "You weren't being nice, you were setting me up. You knew what he wanted." I motioned towards Michael.

"You just don't want the responsibility yourself." He shook his head and explained. "I don't mean to push you. He's right you do smell like a master vampire. He looked at me in a seductive way that suggested he like that I smelled like him. You have the abilities and you need to learn to take on more responsibility. This is as good a place as any to start."

It annoyed me that he didn't warn me about this. I was going to need to think about this. "If I oath him what does it mean exactly?"

Viktor answered my question without sounding triumphant but I could tell he was pleased that I hadn't said no, yet. "You will have a connection to Michael. He will gain some of your characteristics, hopefully good judgment. You will have the ability to control him somewhat. You will know what he is doing and feel if something is wrong. On the other hand you will gain strength from him and he will have to protect you. There are many benefits for you."

I looked at Michael and tried to imagine being responsible for someone else let alone a professional killer. It seemed kind of like adopting a full grown Pit Bull. What if he turns on me? "I don't know. I need to think about this." There was no way I was making a decision like this without time to think it through.

"Please consider this option. I have not been wise in my previous endeavors but I am willing to change. I can't even fathom what I would have done if a child had actually been harmed. I want to make up for that at least. If you decide otherwise I understand." His words were heartfelt but his body language told of the misery in his mind. He almost screwed up royally.

I left the two of them alone and returned upstairs to join Alex. She could tell that something was bothering me and I told her to wait and I would explain later. When we returned home I told her the situation.

"I think you ought to do it. If you oath him he will have to protect you. Frankly I've been worried about you with all the things you're getting into." I hugged her and said goodnight and left to go sleep at the gallery, alone. I wished the flying ability would kick in soon. I could be there in seconds. Instead I drove and ended up parking 3 blocks away since I had let the parking spot go when I moved to my new home. The city was quiet just before dawn and as I passed the dark streets I had a weird feeling. I wasn't sure if it was just all the things on my mind or what. I let myself in and slept in my old safe room upstairs. Skye didn't even wake as I slipped past her sleeping form.

Chapter 36

When I woke I called Viktor. "I'll do it." He didn't respond so I went on. "I need to go pick up our costumes for the parade and then I'll be over." "It's good that you are doing this. You won't regret this decision. See you soon." I was already having regrets though and had to keep telling myself this would be for the good. Michael wasn't a lost cause. He didn't deserve to die for one stupid mistake. It would be good having someone on my side that I knew I could count on. I wouldn't judge him too quickly like Tarik had done to me.

I drove to the costumers and picked up the custom designed outfits for my family and Viktor. We were riding in the parade tomorrow night. When I got to the club I went straight to the office where Viktor was waiting with Michael.

I looked at them both and without so much as a hello I asked Victor: "okay, so how do we do this?" Victor explained that we would each speak the ritual words and then exchange blood. That was all there was to it.

"What if we change our minds?" I asked Viktor just in case something went wrong. "The oath can be transferred to another master vampire if you wish, and they agree. Or you can just kill him." I looked at Michael who slouched sexily on the couch. He was really good at the shabby beach bum thing. "He doesn't have a say in it?" I motioned toward Michael as I asked the question.

"No, he doesn't have a say in anything. He's lucky we didn't just stake him that night. His friends were not so lucky." It was one thing to kill someone in battle or as an assignment but to have to execute a prisoner, well that job just reeks. At least that wasn't my job. Nope, I'm just the babysitter.

"What happens after the oath? Does he have to be near me all the time or anything?" Viktor stifled a snicker at my discomfort. "It's better if he's near you but moving to the city is sufficient. With you being a new vampire you can't sustain a long distance connection like Tarik can. He can't leave the city without your permission. The point is that you have backup, full time so I suggest you keep him close. Michael has a very special gift. He's a day walker, he can stay awake through the day and go out in the sun. Michael can protect you even while you sleep.

I looked at Michael. I guess the tan is real. He smiled and his white, white teeth gleamed. I could see a hint of fang. Either he was nervous or he was showing off. It irked me that I couldn't tell which. "Let's just do this then."

Viktor stood and headed for the door. "You're not staying? What if he tries something?

"I'm sure you can handle him. He either learns to deal with you now or face worse." I wasn't sure how to take that but before I could speak Michael did.

"I'm sure she can handle me and if you're not careful she's liable to handle you too." Viktor just smirked and left through the back door that led to the parking lot. When he was gone I turned to face Michael who had been across the room and on the couch but was now right under my nose.

"Shit!" I jumped back a step. Not very bad ass of me. "You're just full of tricks aren't you?" I glared at him and stepped forward to assert myself. "If we do this you need to behave." Duh, I sounded so stupid even to myself. "Do what I say and keep out of my way. No sneaking up on me. Is that clear?"

"Crystal." He agreed with words but his eyes and lips told another story. What was I getting myself into? I just shook it off and continued on. "Lets' get this over with." I grabbed his hand and led him to the couch where we sat facing each other.

I spoke first and he followed, "My blood to yours, your blood to mine." "Follow as you lead, blood will bind." We continued as Viktor had instructed. It all seemed kind of Ouija Board weird. I could only think that this was just stupid, nothing would happen. How could a few words and a little blood bind two people with absolutely no history?

We each bit into the others wrist and began to drink. Instantly I felt lightheaded and intoxicated. The room spun and I reluctantly licked the wound on his wrist closed even though he was the best thing I'd tasted since Tarik. I forced him to do the same by pulling my wrist away. Watching his tongue slowly drag over my skin seemed like the most sensual thing I had ever seen. The next instant we were all over each other, spread out on the couch. We both wore jeans and as we frantically writhed against each other the pleasure mixed with pain from our clothes chafing. His erection raged against me and the realization of how huge he was just fueled the fire. This was a hell of a strong reaction.

We rolled off the couch and I straddled him on the floor. Michael pulled my t-shirt over my head and was buried in my cleavage when the door opened and Viktor walked back in. He pulled me up and off of Michael by the shoulders and turned me towards him. "I didn't tell you about this. Blood oathing will make you ravenous for each other at first if there is not a dominant enough vampire."

It was like he threw cold water in my face. "What!"

"No, no. It's only temporary. You learn to control it. I knew that you wouldn't do it if you thought something like this would happen."

"No shit! You think?"

"I was waiting right outside. I wouldn't let anything happen. It's no big deal, just a side effect."

"A side effect? What the hell kind of side effect is that? Is it like the pills they advertise for insomnia that cause erectile dysfunction, hair loss, and a anal seepage?"

"Don't get so pissed. It's over, you made it through the worst part. If anyone can hold out it's you."

"Pissed? I'm beyond pissed! You're supposed to be my boyfriend and you tricked me into this situation! You're about to learn how I can hold out. I practically raped him right here in your office." I looked over at Michael who looked a little bit shell shocked. "Damn! I just want to go hump his leg! That's not a side effect, that's a fucking disaster. How am I going to think with him around all the time?"

I walked up to Viktor and poked him in the chest for emphasis. "Don't ever fuck with me again! I have the right to know what kind of shit I'm getting myself into." With that I grabbed my shirt, stomped off and slammed the door for emphasis which was totally wasted when I realized I had to go back for my pet. Shit!"

I opened the door and growled at him. "Are you coming?" He looked around and got up off the floor and walked to the door. This time I refrained from slamming it. When we got out into the parking lot I laid down the rules. Absolutely no touching, looking, or even thinking about it. We drove to my house while I grilled him for info.

"How did you become a rogue. I mean, what makes anyone become a rogue. I just don't understand the concept I guess." "The vampire who turned me died. When that happened I just went sort of nuts. I had no other affiliations, no one to keep me grounded, no purpose in life. I was ready to die too. That's how I became a mercenary. It worked out pretty well until I came here. The people I targeted were all bad guys, drug dealers, hired killers. Then I got mixed up with John and found out how stupid I had been. I deserved what the others got. Why did you save me?"

"I thought you were worth saving. Everyone makes mistakes. Just don't screw up again."

Deja Voodoo

He looked a little worn out and I could understand that. I felt the same way. "Where were you staying before we detained you?" He gave me the name of the hotel and we went there first to get his stuff and check him out. It was not exactly tourist area and kept an eye out for trouble as he gathered his things. On the way to the house I set out some ground rules.

"You can stay in the guest room on the third floor. Don't touch any of my stuff up there. The main loft is where I paint. I sleep downstairs in the safe room. Except for now my sister, Alex and Luke are staying there. I will sleep at the gallery. Since sunlight isn't a problem you don't need to worry. You're there to guard me and in this case my sister and her family. As soon as possible we can arrange for the rest of your things to be moved here and figure out where to put you permanently.

Besides being a watchdog you can help me with stocking the gallery and on the assignments from the council. Occasionally I get assignments that I can't handle on my own so we can work together."

He was being very quiet. "Do you have a problem with any of this?"

He raked me over with those fantastic blue eyes and I stifled a shiver. "I can take orders. I'm especially good when a woman tells me what she needs."

"Don't be a smart ass. I smacked him on the back of the head. Don't even think about touching my AB negative. That's for special occasions. Behave yourself, keep your feet off the coffee table, I made it myself." I kept up with the rules all the way home and parked in the curved driveway on the side of the building. The drive was added after the building was turned into a mortuary and was designed as an entrance for the hearses to load the coffins for burial. Some people think it's weird that I live in an old mortuary but the building is fantastic and somehow it doesn't spook me.

The mortuary is home to nine ghosts that I have met so far. Most of them keep to themselves and stay pretty quiet. The location is convenient because it is close to the cemeteries that I am still helping to restore. I told Michael about them as we entered. "And you will be on a salary, I don't make anyone work for free."

Chapter 37

This night had been crazy so far. I just wanted to get Michael settled and get to the gallery and collapse. Everything was quiet, Stacia and her nanny were asleep already and Alex and Luke were watching a movie. I introduced Michael and we went upstairs and I showed him to the guest bedroom on the third floor. The room was small but had its' own bathroom and a small desk and chair. It would be fine for now and Michael didn't complain.

Before I left he spoke to me. "Don't think I don't appreciate what you're doing for me. I take my responsibility seriously. If you had said no I would be dead now, you know, permanently." I left the mortuary and headed to the gallery. Canal Street was busy even at this late hour due to Mardi Gras.

Deja Voodoo   144

I wound my way through the French Quarter and parked. I gave in to the reality that if you want to park in the French Quarter you either wander the street forever searching or you pay dearly. I could afford it now so I rented a permanent space near the galleryagain. I may be on track to live forever but I don't want to spend it circling blocks for a parking spot. I figured Skye could use it when I didn't. I don't know why I let my old space go anyway.

I let myself in the gallery and flipped through the mail on my desk. There was nothing pressing, utility bills, junk mail, just the usual. I went up the stairs and entered my old room. Skye was sleeping soundly in the bed with a tattooed hunk draped across her. "Nice ass." I mouthed to their sleeping forms. The next evening was the Krewe Ball and I needed some sleep. I locked myself in the safe room after a quick shower and fell asleep instantly.

Chapter 38

When I woke Skye was locking up the shop and heading up to get dressed for the Ball or Bal Masque as it is called in New Orleans. My clothes were here and I had already laid out my elaborate costume. Everyone wore masks and Skye made ours. I wore a black halter gown with a train and trailing sleeves ala Morticia. The dress had a flame design in tiny red beads embroidered on it. The elaborate mask with black and red feathers matched perfectly with the dress and my hair.

Skye wore a crazy retro fifties looking costume and matching mask. Her outfit included a black poodle skirt but the pink poodle was a skeleton. The numerous petticoats made the skirt fluff out and the matching pink and black sweater enhanced her more obvious assets. We rode together to meet everyone at the formal gathering. Luke and Alex arrived shortly after we did and they told me that Michael was staying at the Mortuary with Stacia and the Nanny. We also had two guards outside to keep them safe.

. I was still furious with Viktor and gave him a stony look when he came up to greet me. He wisely backed off and I was glad I wouldn't have to make a scene. When we had a moment alone I told Alex about what happened when I blood oathed Michael. "Oh, you poor little vampire, sexy guys falling all over you. Get over yourself. I agree with Viktor. It's a small price to pay to save someone's life and he did stop anything from happening. Give him a break."

"It's not the lusting after Michael that I'm mad about. It's the fact that Viktor kept it from me and did not give me a chance to make the decision based on all of the facts." She shrugged and left me to go and dance with Luke. No matter what she said I couldn't let this slide. If I didn't stand my ground he would always do shit like this to me. I decided to just put it aside for the evening and have a good time. There were several weeks worth of parties, parades, and fun to keep me entertained. I could deal with him later, and boy did I plan to deal with him.

The Ball was in the Quadroon Ballroom at the Bourbon Orleans Hotel. This was our first year and we were throwing a grand gala to launch the event. Some of the Krewes are so big that they have their Bal Masques in the Superdome and even bring in their floats. Many of those balls have entertainment fit for Hollywood with famous actors and musicians on hand.

This was a big event for us. Many out of town vampires were visiting and Tarik would be here as well. That alone was enough to set my nerves chattering. The ball was just the beginning of a whole schedule of events and parades that make up Mardi Gras. Most of the riders on the float were vampires that paid dearly for a spot. The Bal Masque was also a highly coveted and obscenely priced ticket. Everyone was in costume and the entertainment was unimaginable. Magicians were choreographed with rock stars and awed even the most jaded tastes in a Cirque du Soleil style ensemble.

The ballroom was decorated in the traditional colors of purple, green, and gold. The colors were first chosen in 1872 by that year's Rex, the king. Purple stands for justice, green for faith, and gold is for power. Rex is chosen from prominent businessmen each year. Our Rex this year is Tarik.

The decorations draped walls, chairs, tables, and even extended out on the balconies. There was the traditional King cake, a roll like pastry baked into a circle and iced the colors of Mardi Gras. Inside the cake is a plastic baby Jesus and whoever gets the baby must traditionally provide the King cake the next year. It had to be a tradition contrived by a baker to sell more cakes.

I imagined the magicians performing had to be vampires because they were so fast. The one performing now was really good; I couldn't seem to catch her at anything. She was so fast even with my enhanced vision it was a blur. I was busy watching her when I felt someone watching me. I turned slowly trying not to look like I was looking. Out of the corner of my eye I saw a masked figure hurrying away from me through the crowd. It gave me a weird feeling and so I followed the figure until I lost track of the person. Just as I turned to go back to my table I ran smack into someone.

I looked up and recognized Tarik. Why do I keep doing this? His long black hair was tied in a pony tail and his green eyes sparkled mischievously behind a simple mask. I knew this would happen but it still didn't prepare me for the assault on my senses. He was bound to be here and he certainly would take pleasure in tormenting me. I decided to take the offensive and spoke first.

"Hello Tarik, how are you?" I saw a brief hint of surprise before he recovered and responded. "I'm doing quite well thank you." He was also trying the civilized thing it seemed. "So I hear you have a new pet." He smirked as he asked about Michael. Of course he knew, nothing happens without his knowing. I just nodded and he continued. "It's good, you need backup and your strength is our strength."

"What do you mean by that?" It sounded like I wasn't the only one who would benefit from my alliance.

"Viktor is only as strong as his allies, I have an attachment with you and Viktor that is permanent and will always benefit from your strength. It's kind of a trickledown theory, or up in this case. You and Viktor are the only vampires I have ever made. My alliances have been strictly through oath. I'm quite aware of what the connection entails."

"I believe that's more information of genuine value than I have ever learned from you. Why are you opening up to me all of a sudden?"

"With the new alliance in your life I have decided to quit fighting you. Maybe your right, turning didn't change you it just brought out certain homicidal tendencies."

"Wow, thanks for that backhanded compliment. So now you've decided that I wasn't such a sweet innocent human, just a maniac waiting to be released?"

He looked strained as he tried to explain what he really meant. I knew he had just worded it poorly but it was fun watching him squirm. "I didn't mean to imply that you were or are a maniac. I meant that the things on your agenda haven't changed, just your methods of dealing with them. As a human you might have been on a committee or fight for harsher punishment for pedophiles but as a vampire you hand out justice yourself. I don't disagree with you I just think you need to be more careful about how you choose your targets."

We moved apart as a waiter needed to pass by with a tray laden with drinks. Tarik took my arm and led me to a balcony so we could talk. Being close to him was hard enough but his touching me sent a jolt through my body from head to toe. He was positively scrumptious in a black tuxedo and a simple mask that shadowed his eyes.

"Some of the targets Viktor has given you may not be what he's led you to believe. They were involved somehow but mostly he needed them eliminated for all our safety. Some of your targets simply were threats to Viktor's leadership." I tried to digest what Tarik had just said. I couldn't believe this, not only had Viktor tricked me into the oath with Michael but he may have sent me to kill innocent vampires, or at least not guilty of what I thought. "Does he ever do anything without an ulterior motive?" Tarik looked at me with a sardonic smile on his tempting lips. "No, as a matter of fact he is the most calculated person I have ever known. When you found me you know that it was Viktor who put me there." I nodded for him to continue. "What you don't know is that he waited five hundred years to take his revenge. I was in there nearly a hundred years. Lesser vampires have not survived such torture. He did not care if I made it or not. Your rescuing me just gave him a new target of interest. I won't underestimate him again and now I fear for you as well." "Why didn't anyone look for you while you were missing?" Viktor planned the attack well. I had announced to everyone that I planned to take time off. I had left Viktor in charge and no one knew I was actually missing. While I was away he did a lot of reorganizing in our organization. I'm still trying to clean up some of his mess.

I was in shock from what I had learned. I stumbled back from Tarik. "Thank you for telling me this. I'd rather know the truth even if it is ugly." He made a move towards me and I held up my hand to stop him. I needed space and he let me have it. I left the party and walked to the gallery leaving Sky the Jeep keys to get home with.

The city was packed with tourists and I was feeling drained so I hunted for a meal, or two, or three. I just took enough from each to sustain me and get me through the mood that I was in. My hunting was just like nervous snacking when you're human and you're not hungry, you just try to fill a void. My void was now Viktor. I was so pissed at him, how could I be so stupid? I wanted to just confront him but talked myself out of it and decided to turn the tables instead. As far as I was concerned he was my next target. I might not kill him but he was going to wish he was dead.

My first nibble came from a bouncer on break from his club job. I had learned not to drink from drunks and addicts. The after effects were quite annoying. Before I released him I gave him a mental urge to quit smoking. His blood reeked of nicotine. I chose several more on the way to the gallery. By the time I arrived in my old apartment I was somewhat settled and changed out of my evening gown and into jeans and a t-shirt. I had several hours before dawn so I went into the studio to paint. After a few hours of therapeutic artistic exercise I was ready to sleep.

Chapter 39

The weeks were slipping by and I wanted to spend time with Stacia I went to the house to do just that. Her parents were going out and I told them I would watch her along with the nanny. We played games and even Matthew and Lizzy joined in. I fixed lunch for us and even scarfed down a PB&J sandwich myself. Michael joined us and ate one as well. "I had forgotten how great these things are." Maria took Stacia upstairs for her nap and I was left alone with my "pet" vampire. "I'm going next door to check something out, wanna come?" I asked Michael. I figured I was going to have to get to know him and now was as good a time as any. We left the house and headed down the sidewalk to the cemetery next door.

We entered and I began wandering the rows of tombs searching. "What are you looking for?" Michael asked. "I am trying to see if Matthew and Lizzy might be buried here. From everything I have learned they weren't from the families that lived in the house before it became a mortuary." He stood with his hands in his pockets contemplating this. "So you think this is most likely due to proximity?"

"I guess, it's a possibility." We resumed our search and after a while we found them. Right below the hallway window that faces the cemetery there was a family tome with the names of two children that match. Apparently the kids are twins. Judging from the date that they had died inscribe on the ornate tomb their services might very well have been at the mortuary. I told Matthew of the history of my new home and he agreed. The funerals held when it was the Mc Mahon Mortuary were elaborate and for the very wealthy. Often family members stayed overnight as guests and some services lasted days with no expense spared.

"Look at this tomb it's so beautiful." We stood before the ornate marble façade looking inside the gated mausoleum. There was a beautiful stained glass window at the back which had an angel weeping. The children were the first of the family that had been entombed there. How hard it must have been to build this for those children. I wondered if the extreme grief of their parents had kept them from going on. I planned to work with them after Stacia was gone to help resolve the issues holding them. I had tried to help Daniel to move on but he is such a jaded stubborn ghost there's no talking sense into him.

"Why do you want to help ghosts?" I was perturbed by Michael's question. "Why wouldn't I want to help them? For that matter why wouldn't you, or anyone else want to help?" He crossed his arms defensively.

"I think you are being rather presumptive. How do you know they want or need help crossing over? How are these ghosts really any different than us? Who's to say we shouldn't just move on? We are dead too."

"Wow! You do come up with some questions don't you?" I thought about what he said as we walked to the gate. "Maybe we shouldn't interfere. I guess I am just a busybody or something. I just can't resist trying to help." I told him about Julie and the wedding. Michael laughed and said, "Don't you dare go near my mom the two of you would be an extreme danger to society both live and deceased."

"Hey, watch out buddy or I'll not only talk to her I will help her set you up and have you adopting more kids than Brad and Angelina."

"Don't even think about it. I am a happy bachelor and I plan to keep it that way. Until I became a vampire I wasn't even sociable. Some even considered me a hermit."

"What were you like before you were turned?"

"Back then I was a sailor. I had a charter boat in the Bahamas and I took people on cruises. You know, the barefoot cruises that you see advertised in the travel mags?" I spent some time in Greek isles also. Santorini is the ultimate. I miss the ocean."

"Why did you give it up? I mean, since you can still go out in the daylight." I asked him as we jumped the fence near the gate to return home.

"I was sailing when I ran across the woman who turned me. We met in a bar on the island, one thing led to another and the next thing you know we're off on a romantic sail heading for points unknown. We were out the first night when she attacked me. When I rose it was daytime. I thought it had all been a freaky dream. She was passed out on the bed and I went on deck to get ready to sail. I went back below to check on her in a couple of hours and she hadn't moved. When I touched her to wake her up she was cold as ice. She was dead." I watched him struggle with the tale and could tell how hard it was to tell anyone of such a strange thing.

She just lay there with no visible wounds but absolutely no pulse. I just panicked. I thought what if someone finds me like this, they will think I killed her. The night was twisted but nothing like that. I decided to dump her overboard. When I took her outside she instantly started burning. She woke up screaming and I saw her fangs. I threw her away from me and into the ocean where she still burned even in the water. It only took a few seconds but it felt like forever watching that. I went inside after that and was going to look in the mirror, no reflection. I felt my teeth and definitely I had fangs but what the hell. Why didn't I spontaneously combust like she did? I came to shore and learned how to survive on land. I couldn't very well live the life of a loner when I needed humans for food. I haven't been back since."

It was odd hearing his story. His was so different from my own. I told him how my family had been cursed and that I asked to be turned. We discovered that we had both been turned at around the same time and compared notes.

"I wonder how it is that you can tolerate sunlight?"

"Other vampires have told me that it is not unheard of but very rare to be a day walker. I have not run across another one either."

"You might get to meet one while you're living here. The mayor, John Blake is a day walker." We continued on to the house and went inside. Stacia was awake and playing with the new toys with cartoons blaring in her room. We went into the kitchen for a couple of bottles of blood. To think of all the trouble I had to go through to get some that night I helped Tarik escape and now I just send a text and it gets delivered to my door. The stuff is not bad but fresh is still better. Just the thought of fresh blood made me get all hot and hungry. I looked at Michael and the lust just exploded in my system. I just wanted to gobble him up in every way possible. This was even worse than when I lusted after Viktor. I shook my head to clear my stray thoughts and mumbled an excuse to go check on Stacia.

When her parents returned home I tucked Stacia in bed and kissed her goodnight. As I left the sound of her father reading her a bedtime story warmed my heart. I left the house and hopped on the streetcar for the short ride to the French Quarter. It was a while still until dawn so I took out my frustration on some unsuspecting tourists. Sure folks come to N'awlins, get toasted but watch out for the blood suckers. I chose a slightly inebriated college guy who was foolish enough to lose his friends. His night wasn't going to be so much fun or him. I drank a little and then left him with the unwavering need to get some sleep and study for his trig exam coming up soon. His mother owed me big time.

Chapter 40

The next few evenings we went from party to party and I for one looked forward to the parade just so that everything could end and my nice normal life as a vampire could resume. Besides trying to entertain guests, run the gallery, attend all the activities, I had a new man in my life and he looked to be as distracting as the others. I had to take care of some "commissions" and took Michael along to utilize him in those jobs. It was nice having him like my own personal daytime gopher. I tried to keep from abusing him in more ways than one. I wondered if it bothered him as much as it did me. Any time I was near him I felt like a kid in a candy store. He was just that kind of delicious. It didn't look to me that he was having much difficulty resisting me. Sometimes I got a little bit miffed that he seemed more adjusted than I felt.

We met up at C.C.'s – Community Coffee Shop on Esplanade for an early evening recon of a new set of suspects. These were a pair of really strange ones. The couple lived the poster perfect life on the outside but they delved into the seedy side of life. Not only were they into the kinky stuff they were reported to be suppliers of twisted fantasies for a price. They lived along the beautiful street and we watched them sipping their Lattes like normal people. If something didn't happen soon I was going to have to give up. I hadn't fed yet since we took off so early and I was starving. Coffee just wasn't cutting it, and Michael was looking like dessert.

Just when I was about to give up something happened. In walked the Mayor of New Orleans, John Blake and his lovely wife. I rose and shook hands with him when they came over to greet us. I introduced Michael as a friend. They left us to our coffee and went to order their own. I was shocked when the couple joined our marks.

"I so did not see that coming." I whispered to Michael. "Do you think the honorable Mayor is into the whole wife swap thing?" Michael contemplated them surreptitiously over his steaming brew

"I don't get that kind of vibe from him. But I am picking up something hinky. That guy is definitely off somehow. After they finished their coffee the Mayor and his wife waved goodbye to us and a couple of other patrons.

"Always the politician," I murmured. The couple we were watching rose as if to leave but instead approached us. This could be good, or this could be a disaster. I wondered what they were after. The woman took the lead and introduced them.

"Hello, I'm Adrienne and this is my husband Derrick." She extended her carefully manicured hands and I clasped them with my own ordinary ones. She just oozed predator and wasn't very particular as she seemed to be way into me and or Michael.

"Blake tells us you are the one that painted his wife's portrait." I nodded in agreement and she continued talking. I ignored the fact that I already knew that. With vampires their hearing is exceptional and in such a small place we couldn't help but hear everything they had said.

"We saw the portrait hanging in their bedroom didn't we hon?" She looked to her husband and I followed her gaze appreciating the view. Derrick was off mixed blood with that creamy cocoa skin like the most perfect café au lait. His hair was long and twisted into multicolored dreads which I found fascinating. The most startling thing about him though were his light green eyes. He was obviously gorgeous as a human but being a vampire took him over the top. He eyed me appreciatively as I introduced myself and took his hand in mine. Instead of the expected shake he brought my hand to his lips and gave me a nibble kiss that sent shivers down my spine , and not the good kind.

Adrienne ran her hands over Michael's shoulders in a very familiar manner and he awkwardly introduced himself. I think he felt the uber sexual prowess from them as well. We were there to find out more about them so things were probably progressing perfectly. Adrienne ran her hands through Michael's unruly locks and asked, "You just have to do our portraits, and do you ever do nudes? I almost choked on my coffee and sputtered. "Never before but then again I have never been asked to do one either?"

We talked for a while and they invited us to the event they were attending at the NOMA, New Orleans Museum of Art in City Park. We agreed and left together to walk the mile or so to the museum. There was a midnight opening for the exhibit featuring glass art that I wanted to see anyway. We passed one of the St. Louis cemeteries to our right and I always confuse the numbers. I think this one is number two. The one on Esplanade has some of the most beautiful tombs. We crossed the street to the park entrance and the museum was a beacon of light.

There were spotlights roving the sky as well as thousands of lights in all the trees lining the long drive up to the circular structure. "NOMA has one of the nicest sculpture gardens," I told the group. Derrick told us that he had a cousin who had a piece in the garden and we talked about the art there on the way to the museum. When we entered and began to mingle I noted that the mayor was also in attendance. That was nothing unusual though, many of the noteworthy citizens were there. We wandered the tree floors full of art listening to the jazz music drifting through the building. There was champagne, dancing, and before long I found myself cornered by Derrick as I noticed Adrienne leading Michael down a long gallery.

He prowled more like a lycan than a vampire and kept an arm wrapped possessively around me as we viewed the exhibit. Unnervingly enough we had managed to end up in an alcove that housed some rather erotic nudes. I was uncomfortable but tried not to show it. He leaned in from behind and licked up the side of my neck making me shiver. "You haven't fed properly." He stated the fact as he nibbled my earlobe. Sometimes I have to act bold to get the information or result I needed. I turned in his arms and looked him squarely in the jugular. A little sharing was in order. I bit into him for just a little taste. You can tell a lot about a vampire by the taste of their blood. I drank from him and was intoxicated by his exotic flavor. I got the sexual proclivities and a few other feelings into his psyche. There was nothing alarming in the vibes I got from him. Reluctantly I drew away and sealed the wound with one last swipe of the tongue. I wish it was like with humans, their minds are easy to read.

Our eyes met and his mouth claimed mine and I didn't have to pretend Is it wrong that a potential bad guy rang my bell? Maybe, but maybe he wasn't an actual bad guy either. It could be that he is just your average horny devil. I pulled away from the embrace but kept my hand twined in his. I twirled one of his twisted locks of hair in my other hand and questioned him. "Just what kind of fun can you and Adrienne provide?

"That depends on what your own limits are. Are we up for just a little fun or do we want to get more exotic? I answered him, "What do you consider exotic?" He drew my arm towards him and licked from the wrist to the elbow bend giving me a little nibble. "You my dear are just exactly to my taste. If you are of the mind to share we can explore many opportunities the just four of us." That was obvious in the way they tried to divide and conquer us. What we needed to know was do these two provide more exotic entertainment than what we see now?

Michael and I had decided to lay a trap for these two. We would entice them and pass Michael off as the kind who will go for anything, even the unthinkable. Word was that Adrienne, was as dysfunctional as they come. With a little bait we hoped to find

Leslie Brown

out if they were procurers, people who kidnapped, bought, sold, or traded sex slaves. I wondered how Michael was faring with his target. I insinuated that Michael's tastes were a bit more over the top than my own.

We wandered and flirted through the museum until we met up with the others. Michael seemed to be having quite a time peeling Adrienne off. I couldn't blame her though he was scrumptious. I figured I better rescue him though so I slid into their embrace and kissed Michael like I wanted to devour him. We moved apart reluctantly and gave the pre-arranged excuse simultaneously.

"This has been enticing and we would love to explore opportunities with you at a later date. Unfortunately for tonight though we have a previous appointment that we cannot possibly ignore. We will be at the Baccus Bal Masque tomorrow night, will we see you there? They nodded in unison and bid us goodnight.

When we left we walked around the park and past the many cemeteries around to Canal Street and to the house. The Museum is only a couple of miles from the house and the moon was full. We didn't speak until we were seated in the living room.

"Whoa, that was intense." I uttered as we popped open two bottles of O-positive, Thai blood. We clinked the bottles together and took generous swigs. "I think you got the better end of that deal. At least Derrick was somewhat of a gentleman. I never thought I would get away from her."

He took another swallow and told me what he had learned. "She was a font of information when I could keep her mouth off of me. Apparently she likes anything and everything and the more the merrier. She even mentioned some fun times with Blake."

"Ew, I'm sorry you had the worst end of it. When we go to the party tomorrow we can probably try to set up a play date with them and ask them to step it up a notch."

"I made it crystal clear that I was really into the pre-pubescent girls and that if she wanted me she would have to provide additional entertainment."

"Again, ew! I hate dealing with crap like this but if the end result is going to put away a few freaks then bring it on. I got the vibe that they aren't actually married." Michael agreed, "Yeah, she seems way more out there than he does." I think we can get something out of them in any case. We need to catch the man behind the kidnapped children. So far there had been three.

Michael nodded in agreement and we decided to watch television to de-crepify our minds. "I don't know about you but right about now I could use another bottle, how bout it?"

"I'm good, but thanks." I flipped through some channels landing on the original Willie Wonka and stopped. It was at the part where the boat is going through the psychedelic tunnel.

"I love this movie," Michael said as he kicked off his boots and sat on the couch pulling a blanket over himself. We watched the movie and when it finished I went over to Michael and kissed him on the forehead.

"Thanks for doing this with me." I left him there and left for the gallery. I still had a few hours until dawn and wanted to paint for a while.

Chapter 41

The bal masque was one of the formal events of the season. Everyone with any connections, money, or celebrity status were in attendance. Michael looked divine in the tuxedo. His unruly hair was pulled back and it brought out the strong line of his jaw. I had dressed at the house and we left from there for the ball. My gown was a deep purple and Michael complimented me on it. I wore the minimalistic matching mask and handed Michael a simple one as well in black to match his suit.

We had fed earlier and would be better prepared to deal with Adrienne and Derrick is they showed up. There were several people I knew there and we spoke to a few. I spotted the couple we were targeting on the dance floor and we joined the crowd. Michael held me close and the smell of him was overloading my senses. We danced and kissed and didn't have to pretend the lustful embrace. I had been trying to keep from taking advantage of our alliance and this was making all of that futile. He smelled like heaven and I just wanted to disappear with him but we had a job to do.

I noticed they were working their way closer to us and I was startled when Michael bit into my neck drawing a gasp of ecstasy from me. He pulled away and whispered "Showtime." We danced out of their range and into an alcove for "privacy" when they followed quickly behind us. Michael drew the shoulder of my gown down and was ravishing me with kisses when they interrupted.

"So lusty, it's good to see two people with a healthy appetite." Adrienne purred and we turned to face them. I leaned back into Michael to protect both of us from getting into another one on one situation. "You must agree that Michael has what a woman wants?" I asked Adrienne. "It is good to see the two of you, such spice and variety." I raked Derrick with my gaze. "We are planning a party for next week," Michael explained. "An intimate get together with a few of our closest friends. We would love for you to come."

"That sounds intriguing," replied Adrienne as she ran a hand down Derricks arm possessively. "Is this a party for sharing?" Derrick asked while undressing me with his eyes. I returned the interest and said, "Definitely, as a matter of fact we would love to have some special guests. Michael is so particular though. I'm sure we will never find anything to his tastes. He may not join in at all if he doesn't get what he wants." I pouted for emphasis.

Adrienne took the bait and offered, "We may know someone who is able to provide anything you wish." Derrick looked at her with one of those what the hell looks.

"Don't be a bore darling, you know I have friends with very specific tastes." He rolled his eyes at her and said, "I know. It's just that they can be so demanding. The supplier is very expensive, and it's such short notice. We can't promise anything." Adrienne looked like she would do anything to get what she wanted. "I'm sure that money is not a problem, is it?" She aimed that question squarely at me.

Deja Voodoo   160

"Absolutely not, whatever it takes to keep my man happy. As a matter of fact just set everything up and let me know how much it will cost. I know how entertainment can be these days and we are pressed for time."

We agreed to meet the next evening to get them the money for the "entertainment." Adrienne managed to insinuate herself into Michaels space and promised him she would make him a happy boy. From where I was standing I was sure her hand was evaluating just how happy he could get. I dodged Derrick's attempt at seduction and called to Michael to leave. "Let's go darling; I have a surprise waiting for you at home." They reluctantly let us leave and we wound around and through the crowded ballroom and out the doors into the busy streets.

"God; I just want to take a bath when I escape from her. That is one dirty girl." Michael complained as we walked the French quarter. "Suck it up. It's for a good cause. Don't forget that the man you were stupid enough to get involved with is probably they're supplier." He looked haunted when those words sunk in and I was almost sorry I had said them but it was too late to take it back. "Sorry." I offered lamely.

We hunted down some friendly donors, had a warm meal and headed back to the house. I went downstairs to change and Michael headed up. When I was more comfortable in cut off denim shorts and a tank top I undid my hair from the complicated up do my sister had helped me with. I went upstairs to check on Stacia who was sound asleep with her nanny next door presumably doing the same. I was spending the night there since Luke and Alex were on a quick side trip to a nite-surfers competition in Florida. There was a storm in the gulf so they hopped a plane to the keys. I left my sleeping niece and padded downstairs barefoot.

I made some popcorn and grabbed a water bottle to settle down to watch a movie. The Blue Ray player had great quality and I love all kinds of movies. I had a huge variety to choose from. Tonight I chose an older movie that was one of my favorites, Long Kiss Goodnight with Gina Davis and Samuel L. Jackson. It's a great movie with a strong ass kicking heroine protecting her child. It was just right up my alley and as the movie started Michael joined me on the couch and helped himself to my popcorn.

I was not able to enjoy the movie as much as usual though due to distraction. Beside me on the couch Michael sat in a pair of sweats and shirtless. I kept sneaking looks at his irresistible chest and washboard abs. His skin was tanned and smooth with only a teasing trail of hair that disappeared into the sweatpants. It had been weeks since he had moved in and I had quit seeing Viktor I was feeling way too on edge. It would have been easier to resist if he had tried to make moves on me but he never did. It was driving me crazy. I didn't think that the attraction was just because of the binding. He certainly didn't seem bothered by it.

When we were playacting for Adrienne and Derrick we kissed and had some intimate contact but that was just for show. I was not thinking sanely is all I can attribute it to but without over thinking my decision I turned to him and slid closer. I slid my hands on either side of his cheeks with one hands threading its way into his hair as I kissed him. At first he seemed startled but quickly he began to pull me into his embrace and kissed me back. He leaned into me and we ended up lying down on the couch with him on top. My fingers played with the muscles along his back. We kissed and nibbled and explored tentatively. He pulled away and our eyes met.

"I don't want you to do this because of the blood oath," he said.

"I won't do this because of the oath. Why haven't you tried anything since we have been tied together?"

He looked down at me and reached to brush aside a lock of my hair. His thumb brushed across my lower lip and the look he gave me was so full of need. "I had to wait until you were ready to come to me freely. I knew that if I pushed you I would forfeit any chance I would ever have and maybe our friendship."

It was amazing; the men in my life were so complicated. Tarik was just unattainable and stubborn, and Viktor was ever present and manipulating. I was constantly dodging them and right in front of me was someone who gave me the space I needed. He didn't invade my mind although I think he could if he wanted. In all the time we had been oathed he had behaved impeccably. Viktor even confessed to me that the oath I shared with Michael had been exceptionally deep. Ordinarily the two people oathed could take or leave each other after the initial ceremony, but for us the desire had not receded. I decided to test our connection and sent him a mental message.

The picture I willed to him was of us naked together in my bed. I sure hoped this got to the right person. I wasn't very god at this yet and it would be way embarrassing if the message went astray. Apparently the message got to its intended recipient. Michael's eyes spilled from the blue of the sea to pure black and he sent me a message back that made me come undone inside. I pulled him down and we explored each other timidly, neither one of us wanting to screw this up. No pun intended. We made out like kids in the back seat of their parents car. We kissed so much that my lips were raw and swollen and I'm sure his were too. I rolled him over so that we switched positions and I was on top. He was like catnip I swear. I could just roll and rub all over him. I sucked the ring dangling from one of his nipples into my teeth and nicked the skin with fangs, finishing off by licking my way down.

Michael pushed me back and rolled my shirt up to taste my exposed breasts while playing with the piercing in my navel. He let the fabric slide back down and I rose tugging him up with me. We giggled and played all the way down to my room, stopping along the way several times. I reached down his back and into the sweatpants to grab his ass with both hands grinding him into me. He slid my shirt off and let it fall to the floor. We got halfway down the stairs and almost didn't get any farther. When we got to my room I kicked the door shut and followed his sweats to the floor in order to taste my way down his body. I faltered for a moment when I was faced with the enormity of him. I silently sent a thank you to whatever god had made this magnificent man and placed him in my life.

I rose and slid my own shorts and panties down so that he could appreciate me as well. I was always built well but again the vampire transformation enhanced that. My ample chest was perpetually perky and my derrière would make a Kardashian cry. Michael growled low in his throat and lifted me onto the bed. We took our time and slathered each other with kisses and love bites finally sliding together naturally.

The rhythm he set was just this side of frantic. We switched position and with my ankles high up on his shoulders he drove himself in deeper and harder. The erotic torture almost made me pass out and finally I screamed my release as he did simultaneously. He drew away and rolled me into his arms protectively. After a while he rose and locked the mechanism that rendered the room safe from daylight. I went to the fridge which happened to be an old row of cadaver chambers. "Hey it works, don't judge." I said when I saw the look on his face when I opened a door and slid out the cadaver drawer. I pulled out four bottles of the good stuff. I removed the lids and popped them into the microwave for a quick warm up.

I handed him one and took one myself watching him down half the bottle in one swallow. Apparently we were of the same mind. The night was young and we had a lot of exploring to do. I crawled into the big bed and pulled up the covers to cocoon us in as we drank. I climbed on top of him and rode him like I had wanted from the first moment I had laid eyes on him. We made love in so many ways I lost count and eventually succumbed to the pull of dawn. My last thoughts were how this worked for Michael; did he sleep like the dead?

I woke the next night to find him waiting for me. There was warm blood by the bed but I wanted him. I crawled over to him and sank my teeth into the sensitive spot along his groin. He drank the bottled stuff while I fed and watched him grow. I pulled my fangs out and licked my way to my goal. He was delicious and I couldn't get enough of him. We were like rabid bunnies and the mood carried over for our meeting with Adrienne and Derrick where we couldn't keep out hands to ourselves. We planned to meet them at a local jazz club frequented by vampires. We tend to stick to our own kind as much as possible. With all the popularity from movies and books it is hard to fly under the radar. Whenever anyone suspects anything you can just fake like you're a wannabe.

We took the street car down Canal Street and to the riverfront getting off at the last stop by the French Market. Even

Deja Voodoo

near midnight there were a lot of riders and hours were extended due to Mardi Gras. The club we were going to was on Frenchman Street, just on the edge of the French Quarter. We crossed to Decatur and followed it to Frenchman and all of the clubs were in full swing. This area is a semi-hidden jewel of the city. If you want to listen to good music and avoid the tourist traps this is the place to be. The area is called Faubourg Marigny and is an eclectic mix of young up and coming professional's residences to off the beaten path bed and breakfast hotels.

Check Point Charlie's if one of the first places we passed and the music flowed from its doors. The joint actually has a Laundromat in back. When we entered the club there was a female vocalist stirring up the crowd with a soulful melody. We made our way to the back and joined our targets who were already there. I was wondering if Adrienne had accidentally put her dress on backwards, it just looked wrong but in a way the guys must love.

We greeted them with air kisses on each cheek and sat at the remaining two chairs at the pub height table. The club was busy but not crowded so bad that you had no space. Even though it was not overcrowded it was noisy. We agreed to follow them into the courtyard in back. The music still followed but the area was separated enough that we could at least talk.

"The arrangements have been set in motion. We will have entertainment procured that we hope will please you." Adrienne all but purred the information. She was some kind of desperate to make Michael happy.

"If you have the funds ready we can just finish the arrangements." Derrick got straight down to business.

Michael pulled a hefty envelope out of the interior pocket of his jacket and handed it to him. Derrick put the envelope into his own jacket without even a cursory glance inside. It's not like we would try and cheat them. They had what they thought we wanted. Now it was time to set a trap.

"We want to invite your source to our little get together. I am sure someone with his taste and ability would be a coveted asset to our group." We told them when and where the event would take place and insinuated just how warped it would get.

Michael said; "We have been procuring fresh food from near and far, trust me there will be no leftovers." In other words we had expendible humans to consume and discard.

"The feasting should only be surpassed by the entertainment." I added to his description.

"Excellent, we will get this to him and be in touch with you for the details." Derrick told us as he rose and came around to me on the other side of the patio table.

"I look forward to feasting with you my dear." He leaned in close and licked my neck as he passed around to take Adrienne by the arm. She had taken the chance to sidle up to Michael and straddle one of his legs to rub against him like a cat. Derrick led her away before she could molest Michael any further. They left the courtyard by the back gate and we waited just a minute before following.

They would become suspicious if they saw us so we had to be very careful. The couple jumped into their car and we spotted a cab so we got in and followed discretely. We offered the driver a huge tip if he kept up but didn't get spotted tailing them. He eyed the folded hundred dollar bills and took off with determination. We ended up in front of a familiar mansion.

"Ain't that the mayor's place?" The driver asked. We idled just down the street and when the driver took his money we got out and stepped into the shadows of a tree to watch. Adrienne and Derrick got out of the car and entered the house through the front door. We waited and watched for several hours before the two emerged, Adrienne was locked in the arms with none other than Mrs. Mayor. They kissed and pawed each other to the point where I thought they would either jump each other right there or go back inside. Derrick pulled his errant lover away and led her down the steps to the car.

"This wasn't truly helpful," I said as we walked toward St. Charles Avenue to catch a cab home. "We know they have something going on with the mayor and his wife but do they fit into the ring that kidnaps potential sex slaves?" Michael hailed a passing cab and before we got in he said; "I don't care if he's the mayor. If that man has something to do with this he's going to pay." I agreed and we got in the cab and gave the driver directions.

The last few parties were winding down and the final parade would be the next evening. Alex and Luke were back and we went to the gallery. Michael walked me to the door and kissed me good night. I would have to go to bed soon. I had an answer from him about his sleeping habits. He did not have to sleep during the day but he kept the same hours as most vampires just for continuity. Michael left me to go up and walked back to the mortuary-house.

Chapter 42

I woke to screams and pounding on the door. Skye was yelling for me to get up and I bolted like a madwoman in fear. The door was locked and I fumbled for the heavy lock and punched in the codes for the electronic controls. Skye fell in on me while she breathlessly told me what was wrong. "Stacia's been kidnapped, the mortuary was attacked and the nanny was killed. Luke and Alex were unharmed because they were in the safe room but Michael was gravely injured. It looks like Were's did it. The place was ransacked and the guards were shredded to pieces. Everyone is meeting there now."

I threw on some clothes while running out of the room and down the stairs. It had to be the kidnaper that was behind it. It was revenge for spoiling his last plan. All the way to the house I

Leslie Brown   167

was going through the scenarios in my head. Even my worst imaginings paled in comparison to the reality. The guards had been taken inside and slaughtered on the spot. There was blood and gore everywhere. At least we had a chance to keep this from the local police. They were smart enough to keep the carnage inside. The building is secluded and no one living would have heard their screams.

As I walked through the building the ghosts scampered after me all talking at once telling me everything. It was the same thing as before, a child had been kidnaped The ghosts had heard them talking about what they planned for Stacia. The kidnaper was going keep her until she was the perfect age, six and then turn her for himself. This was his revenge for my interfering in his business.

Tarik and Viktor were on their way and Alex was furious. I ran to her and grabbed her arms to still her frantic pacing. "I will get her back. Don't be afraid. She will be alright." She rolled her eyes at me and roared. "He's mine! I'm going to devour him whole! How dare he take my baby?" She resumed pacing and Luke tried to calm her. In between pacing she glared at me with accusing eyes. I knew it was my fault. If I hadn't gotten messed up in this Stacia would never have been taken. Luke told me to check on Michael. "He's in bad shape, I don't think he'll make it." I left them and went in search of Michael.

He was upstairs in the room Stacia and her nanny had shared. What was left of the nanny lay in pieces on the floor and bed. To think that Stacia had seen this brutality enraged me even more. He was going to pay for this. This guy was going to die screaming.

Michael lay on the floor in a bloody heap. I knelt beside him and gently turned him on his back. He had a huge gash across his stomach and many smaller ones all over. It looked like he had been thrown against the wall. It must have knocked him out and that had saved his life. If he wasn't a vampire he would have died already. As it was he was barely holding on. As I examined his wounds Tarik and Viktor arrived and they both took in the scene and exchanged grim looks. Tarik knelt beside me and put an arm around me. I didn't realize that I had been crying until

Deja Voodoo

he spoke. My shoulders shook as he stilled them. I screamed, No!" I looked around at all the carnage in this innocent child's room.

"Save your anger. Hold it inside, you will need it later. There's nothing you can do for him, just let him go." "No, there has to be something!" I roared. Victor approached and spoke. "There is something." Tarik lunged for Viktor and grabbed him by a handful of shirt. "Just leave it! He's not worth it."

I looked at both of them and realized that I was missing something. "What?" I looked at Tarik. "What is it that you don't want me to do?" Viktor pushed Tarik back and told me what I needed to know. It was getting very annoying to be the last one in on the joke every time. He came forward and told me, "You can save him. The question is do you want to pay the price." I looked them both with distrust and asked. "What do I have to do? He nearly died trying to save my niece! Just tell me what!"

Tarik turned and said, "I can't be a part of this." As he stormed out of the room I thought of all the times he had left when I needed him. I looked over to where Michael lay dying and had to wonder. What was in it for Viktor? Was he actually just caring about someone or would this serve some demented purpose for him. "Spit it out. What do you get out of helping him?" He smiled and said, "It's always nice to be thought so little of by those you care about so deeply." I glared at him and said, "Cut the crap! What do I have to do and how will this benefit you." He sauntered around the room looking smug and answered. "The choice is purely yours. Let him die or save him. I don't really care either way. Whichever you chose I win. Let him die and I watch your morals slide into oblivion. Save him and watch my brothers tortured heart. Looks like a win-win situation to me."

I roared at him, "You arrogant ass! Why did I ever fall for your lies?" He smirked and posed against the blood drenched corpse of the nanny. "I never lie; you just fail to see the truth."

"What do I have to do?" I eyed him suspiciously as he came closer. "Just feed him your blood to help him heal. With your bond you are the only one he will respond to as weak as he is."

"And then what happens? I know that can't be all because nothing is ever so simple where you're concerned. Tell me everything."

"As you wish, the knowledge will make the torture all that sweeter. When you feed him he will heal. With the amount of blood he will need there is a danger that he will drain you dry. If you somehow manage to avoid that then you will have to feed from him and that will bind you even closer. At the very least you will ravage each other. Worst case scenario he kills you and then follows. Either way it's your choice." With that he walked out and left me with Michael.

"Alex!" I yelled for her to come and she was there in seconds followed by Luke. "Help me get him to my room. I have to try and save him but I need your help." Luke lifted Michael like he weighed nothing even though I knew he had to top 250lbs. He was Six feet four of pure muscle and made his living with that muscle, if you subtracted the blood loss though he was a little lighter. We descended the three flights of stairs carefully to avoid moving him too much. Inside my safe room Luke laid him on the bed. Alex said, "What do you need?" I explained what would happen and told them to just let me begin to feed him and if it got out of control do what they had to. I would try to save him but I wasn't taking any chances.

I crawled onto the bed beside him and felt for his pulse but it was very weak. I looked at Alex and used my own fangs to open a wound on my wrist for him to drink from. I held my arm to his mouth but he just lay still. "Don't die on me! Drink!" I shook him and tilted his head back like you would for mouth to mouth resuscitation but instead squeezed blood from my wrist into his mouth. His mouth filled and he began to cough spraying blood all over me. With a gasp his eyes flew open and he latched onto the bloody wound and began to drink.

Relief poured over me as he swallowed more and more. I relaxed and lay down beside Michael as he drank. With each drop I felt him gain strength as I weakened. My mind began to get fuzzy and I couldn't remember what it was I was supposed to do. Alex shoved a bag of blood into my other hand and I bit into it sucking the bag dry in one hit. I kept fresh bags in case of an

Deja Voodoo

emergency and this definitely qualified. Luke kept passing her bags and I kept draining them. There were several cadaver drawers to keep them cold. After the last bag was drained I began to regain some ability to focus. He was draining me even with the blood I was replacing.

I looked at his body and the huge gash had healed. I looked at his eyes and saw that he was getting blood drunk. If I didn't stop his feeding he would kill himself with it. Sucking me dry was not an option either. I held his head with one hand and tore my wrist away. He lunged after me and tried to pull it back. Luke and Alex grabbed his hands and arms and held him down. With all my strength I held his head still and I bit down hard on his jugular vein. I felt him surrender to me as I drank. The blood equalized us both and I was finally able to think clearly. I pulled back and realized that I had straddled his body. He lay calm so Alex and Luke released their holds but stayed close just in case.

He looked fine except that he was covered in drying blood and shredded clothing. I felt along his arms for the wounds that were no longer there. My fingers trailed over his upper arms and over his smooth chest. The wounds were completely healed. I peeled away the remnants of his shirt to reveal his healing skin. It was still red and you could see a line where the mortal wound had been. I bent down and trailed my tongue over the temporary scar. In minutes it would be gone.

Our eyes met as I crouched over his body. The lust flowed over us like an avalanche. I growled and lunged for his mouth with my own. Oblivious to the other people in the room I rubbed myself against him like he was vamp catnip. What was left of his pants couldn't contain his own enthusiasm. I rubbed against the hard length of him unable to stop myself. I licked my way down to free him from the annoying cloth. The sound of the door shutting registered and I guessed that we had been left alone. At that point I was so far gone I didn't even care. Michael writhed as I took him in my mouth, fangs grazing him without restraint. In a blur he flipped me on my back and my clothes were flung in every direction. His fangs pierced my skin again and he licked the wound closed as he shoved inside of me. It wasn't sex it was a violent possession on both of our parts. We each took and took some more.

Leslie Brown   171

What must have been hours had gone by and we were finally under control enough to think. Michael spoke first as we finally lay still. "They took Stacia." I put my hands to his lips "I know. You nearly died trying to save her." He looked around and I could see everything registering on his mind. He looked at me and that look almost broke my heart. He thought he had failed, he thought he wasn't worth what I had done to save him again. I wondered what had happened to him that he would think so little of himself. I would have to find out but this wasn't the time. I rolled over and slid my leg over his. The movement brought us eye to eye and I spoke. "You're definitely worth it." The lascivious grin on my face brought a smile to him and it almost reached his eyes. Those beautiful eyes remained sad. We rose and showered in silence knowing that there was a battle ahead. "It was John Blake, the mayor. He's the one behind this." What Michael said registered. Because of our attempts to trap him we had become the target. Blake knew who I was and was paying me back for taking away the other child. Now he had taken my niece.

Chapter 42

Michael went upstairs wrapped in an oversized towel to get some clothes and I dressed quickly. We met in the living room and apparently we had been at it for a while. The corpses were gone and the blood was gone. The furniture that wasn't destroyed was righted and the room looked almost normal. Viktor had the best cleaners in the city. The room was full of vampires and all of them turned to me as I entered the room. How embarrassing, the hostess was late to the party because she was knocking boots with the hired help.

Viktor looked smug as he sat in my favorite chair. "Oh get over yourself!" I stormed over to him. "While you're at it get out of my chair!" He laughed but did as I said and I plopped on the cushy surface. I felt like a petulant child but it was my house and I was really pissed. What made it even harder was that he didn't make the rules he just told me how to play. He had been right and I had to choose. Now I had to live with that choice. Being a vampire sucks sometimes.

Michael came into the room and I watched him like he was an all you can eat buffet. I couldn't help myself. I was so never going to live this down. Viktor was holding his side and almost crying from the attempt to not cackle at us. I ignored him and was glad that Michael had enough sense to sit across the room. "It was Blake, the mayor. Michael told me that he heard them talking when they came in and took Stacia and they thought he was dead."

"Lets' go get him!" Alex lunged out of her seat like she would do it. Viktor spoke and for once I was in agreement with him. This wasn't just some low life we could go and grab. This was the mayor of a large city. People would notice if he disappeared and we couldn't just barge in at city hall.
"We have to be careful; we can't spook him and let him know that we know it is him. We need to watch him and find out where he's keeping her or at least figure out a way to snatch him without being caught.

Alex spoke at last. "There is no way we will find Stacia on our own. We know John has her so the logical thing to do is get him to give her back." I looked at her like she was a simpleton. "I know, I know. He isn't just going to give her back. We have to persuade him but we can't get close to him without setting off alarms." Viktor stood and added, "We can get him at the parade tonight. He's riding on a float with the Saints cheerleaders. He won't expect an attack from them."

I rose and paced the floor. "Just how are we supposed to get the Saints cheerleaders to help us kidnap him?" He closed in on me and grinned. "We replace the cheerleaders with vampires." He looked so smug I had to knock him down a peg. "He can smell a vampire a mile away; we will never pull it off." Viktor sat back down on the couch and spoke. "I have a little something that can fix his sense of smell. My lab has come up with a scent masking solution. We drench the ladies and take him tonight. If you wish

I will even let you torture the information out of the mayor yourself."

"Gladly" I replied knowing I had just slid into another of Viktor's manipulative schemes. This one was non-negotiable and worth the cause. I would do anything to save my niece and get that slime bucket off the streets. The plan was to hijack the float and replace the cheerleaders with our own girls which were already in place. We had to act fast to do it though. The group divided up and piled into cars. We drove to the staging area for the parade and met up with the new and improved not so saintly cheerleaders as they got on the float. Their float was set to roll right in front of ours and we would be close enough to see the action. The honorable Mayor would also feel safe with us occupied where he could keep an eye on us.

The mayor arrived with his entourage and eyed us smugly as he got on the float. He flirted appropriately with the girls but kept it clean. He has to keep up the public opinion of an honest politician by not slobbering over the girls. The scent mask seemed to be working and he was not at all alarmed. We rode through the streets throwing beads and baubles like there was nothing wrong all the while watching him. It was hard to watch him so close and pretend that we knew nothing. The few miles of the parade route drug on like we were moving in slow motion. Michael and I positioned ourselves at the front of the float each atop the lead horses pulling the antique hearse. The horses were bigger than life and they lunged forward like demon horses, ebony manes flying, red eyes glowing in LED lights. The graveyard loomed behind them with all manner of characters hanging out of the tombs. There were vampires, zombies, lycanthropes, ghosts and all of them were real. The scary factor was doubled with the fierce determination steeling us all for the fight to come. We travelled through the crowds throwing beads waiting for the parade to end.

The parade wound down through the Garden District to its final destination at a warehouse along the river on Tchoupitoulous Street. My mouth was frozen into a fake smile and my arms were numb from throwing beads. As the floats approached for parking the one in front of the Mayor led the way to a new building. After our float entered the line was cut off sending the remaining floats to another warehouse. The three floats took up most of the space and what Blake didn't know was that we were on all three floats. He was surrounded with nothing but enemies all ready to rip him to shreds.

I approached the float from behind and as he saw me the look on his face said it all. The cheerleaders bared their fangs and I jerked him off of his paper mache throne. "Don't ever fuck with my family!" I threw him over the edge and jumped over to follow. He crouched there and spit blood onto my new boots. That really pissed me off. I crushed the fingers on his right hand with the heel of those same boots. "Where is she?"

He just glared at me and said, "You'll never find her." I leaned down into his twisted face and whispered, "Oh goody, I always liked the hard way." A limo pulled up and we threw him in the trunk. Viktor, Michael, Alex, Luke, and I got in and we sped off. The mansion we often used was nearby and we took him there. The driver was very good and we made it through the narrow, crowded streets quickly.

We got John inside and tied him to the sunroom bed. It was the same room I had fried numerous bad vampires on Viktor's order. I wondered how many had been innocent. This one certainly wasn't though.
With a push of the button the same lights that people lay under for a glowing tan become lethal weapons against vampires. That was too fast for him though. I wanted him to suffer. And I want the information I need to save Stacia. Luke and Alex tried to follow us into the room but I stopped them. "You don't need to see this." I didn't need to see what I was reflected in their eyes.

I went to the drawer and slid it open revealing an array of weapons. I pulled out a finger knife. I turned and made a show of sliding it over my fingers and I grasped the hilt with my palm. "A perfect choice when you don't want the blood to make you lose your grip." The blade glinted in the light as I turned it in the air. He looked at me with hatred and arrogance. "I didn't know you thought of me in that way. Blood is such an aphrodisiac." He grinned cruelly as he spoke. Just great, he was even more sadistic than I thought. I held the knife to his groin and threatened. "I'll cut off something that won't grow back." He actually had the good sense to pale a little and swallow a smart assed comment.

Viktor walked over to the dresser and pushed a button on the laptop that was opened there. The screen came to life and a counter ticked numbers away one digit at a time. Blake finally looked worried. "What is that?" Viktor smiled and looked at me. "You have so much to learn grasshopper. If you want to torture information out of someone you need to have a weapon that they actually fear." I stared at the screen and watched the numbers dwindling. "This is all of Mr. Blake's money disappearing into nothing. I have accessed all of your accounts and not just the legitimate ones. With every second that ticks by your money is evaporating into random charities across the globe. On the bright side that's one hell of a tax deduction. Oh, look there goes another hundred thousand. I think that one goes to clothe the Chihuahuas or something, how very generous of you. I didn't take you for a purse dog kind of guy"

The sound that came out of Blake was very much like the one a lion does when you take away its dinner. I had been perfectly willing to slice and dice the info out of him but thanks to Viktor's deviant mind I wouldn't have to. What a pity. The only thing that surprised me was that he didn't make me go through with it just a little bit. It made up just a little bit for the thing with Michael. Viktor told him what we wanted, namely Stacia.

"Give us the child unharmed and you will not have to lose your money. I'm sure the race for governor is getting quite expensive. I'd hate for you to have to loose due to a lack of advertising funds."

He looked genuinely concerned as he teased Blake. "I hope you don't have her stashed too far away. It would be a shame if all your money just disappeared before you get her to us. Get her home in time and you might just be able to keep a small fortune." Viktor dialed the number Blake gave and put the phone up to him so he could talk. "It's Blake, take the girl back home. No. Just do what I say! Make it fast; your ass depends on it. If she's not back immediately you're a dead man." That was a nasty one sided conversation if I ever heard one. Viktor clicked the phone shut and I ran to the door yelling orders.

Deja Voodoo

"Michael! Take Alex, Luke and a half a dozen men to my house. If Stacia's not back in fifteen minutes call me so that I can begin the real torture."
I looked back at the room that held John Blake and was disgusted by his depravity. The things he would have done to my niece were unthinkable. He had killed my friends and almost killed Michael. I had a little time to kill so I decided to get some questions answered. I went in and shut the door so that it was only me and Viktor with John again. I knew that Viktor wouldn't stop me. At this point I didn't care. I was tired of chasing scum like this to the ground.

"I should just go ahead and kill you now. Why wouldn't I?" He never took his eyes off the computer screen. That gave me an idea. I leaned over him to block the view of the screen.

"How about for every name you give me I give you back one million dollars of your money. That sounds fair. I let one perv live but I get dozens more. I can live with that. What do you say?" For emphasis I lifted his chin with the knife blade I still held. Blood pooled on the razor sharp edge and dripped off onto his pristine shirt.

"How do I know you won't kill me anyway or that you will put back the money?" I grinned at him and said, "You will just have to trust me. After all, I'm not a sleazy politician like you." He blurted out a name. Viktor shrugged and typed something into the computer and the money began to roll back into the accounts.

"Technology is such a wonder." I said and backed away from Blake. "How do I know you are giving me real names?" He squirmed and said, "Look in my Blackberry. The password is 34skip67." I dug in his pocket and pulled out the device handing it to Viktor. He messed around with the little gadget for a minute and then whooped out loud. "It's the motherload! All the big name creeps in America, sexual preferences and all. There must be a hundred names in here. You're going to need this money to make yourself invisible when word gets out it's you who leaked this information."

My cell phone rang and I answered. "Is she there?" Michael told me they had her. I replied, "Take out his men." After I hung up the phone I turned to Viktor. He closed the computer and left the room. Blake began screaming. "You promised, you promised!"

"I made a promise to myself first." I went over to him and planted my fist into his smug mouth. "That was for me." I sliced the knife across his belly like the wound inflicted on Michael. "That was for Michael, and this is for Stacia and the other children." I walked out of the room to the sound of his screams, shut the door, and clicked the remote in my pocket to switch on the lights. The screams stopped.

Chapter 43

Alex, Luke, and Stacia went home. I wondered if they would ever visit me again. I began to cross the names off the list from Blake's Blackberry with the help of Michael and Viktor. I had decided to work with Viktor on this but only because I knew he wasn't feeding me false information. All of the people on this list were legitimate freaks. It was kind of strange working together but we all had the same agenda. We didn't look at each other's motives we just got the job done.

I had to get on with my life, wherever it took me. Michael and I just accepted each other. Viktor is the necessary evil in my life. I can't trust him but I know he has my back. If I'm not careful he is liable to nail it again. The man never gives up. Tarik is just there. No matter where I am I feel him. I don't think I will ever be what he needs but I am what he wants. For now, this life works for me. I looked down at the printout from the blackberry. I wondered where to start first? The names encompassed six countries. I read down the list and found a familiar name and circled it.

Read an excerpt from the sequel to **Deja Voodoo**......

Bad Moon Rising

He looked up at the full moon and then back down at his prey. For a tiny instant his victim saw a glimmer of humanity in those half human eyes under the light of the moon. Like a curtain being drawn all conscience left those orange and copper orbs. Saliva glistened off his long fangs as he leaned in for the kill.

Sirens blasted loud and garish like the splashes of blood that still lay drying on the banquette. The New

Orleans Police Department Homicide Division was plastered on the side of several cars blocking off the odd spectator or two. The sun had just come up and some unfortunate bartender had come upon the grisly scene on his way home from a late shift. This was a nasty piece of work and far from the normal crime scene. Day to day life in the city is never without the 2-3 gangbanger style shootings. Those were normal; this was nowhere near normal if you could imagine a murder scene as normal. The victim had been hacked to pieces.

Kat sat curled up on a lounge chair on her balcony of her art gallery overlooking Royal Street. She was drinking her morning java, well actually morning to her but to the crowds ambling by it was a brisk Friday night in October. It had been three years since she had died, or rather metamorphosed into the undead. When the only way to remove a deadly family curse was to become undead the choice is easy. Death did nothing to curb her addiction to coffee; on the contrary it had become worse. With plentiful supplies of donated blood in tidy little plastic bags she never had a hunger that vampires of years gone by had to deal with. Kat had a successful art gallery, a beautiful home, (renovated mortuary- don't judge) and a secret career as the undead equalizer what more could a girl wish for? Possibly an uncomplicated love life..

Kat read the day's headlines in the Times Picayune and noted there had been another bizarre killing. She planned to go and see Viktor tonight and would find out what he knew about it. Viktor was her former lover and the brother of her Sire, Tariq. The jury was still out on whether she and Tariq could ever have a "normal" relationship after she forced him to turn her. He just needed to lighten up. Sure she tricked him into doing the deed but she had no choice. If she hadn't done it her sister would be dead right now and not just undead. No matter how many times Kat explained this to Tariq he remained stubborn and refused to forgive her. That didn't stop him from wanting to come by once in a while to try and get in her coffin though, so to speak. From her experience Kat figured vampires could afford to hold a grudge for a very long time, duh.... immortal. Viktor locked Tariq in a silver draped coffin for over a hundred years on just such a grudge. That was how Kat found Tariq, set him free and got him to finally agree to turn her, given the circumstances though she didn't have a choice. Over a century before a Voodoo Priestess cursed her family. Every generation would suffer without love under the curse. The females of the family would know love briefly, get pregnant upon losing their virginity, give birth to a girl and die immediately after. Kat and her twin sister Alex ended the curse by becoming immortal; you can't kill someone who's already dead.

Since being changed Kat continued her life as an artist and gallery owner but soon became involved with Viktor eradicating the scourge of the city. If you think rapists and pedophiles are bad throw in the immortality and supernatural factor and that goes to unfathomable. A vampire child can be tortured indefinitely without aging. For that kind of evil there is no judge or jury, just me and the others who work with Viktor erasing those bastards from existence on our world.

Viktor is the head of the supernatural community of Louisiana; from Loup-Gareau otherwise known as werewolves to vampires, and the occasional faerie. Ghosts seem to have chosen Kat as their unofficial mascot/mediator. Zombies are a whole other matter and only listen to the one who raises them. In New Orleans the job of keeping all of this otherworldly activity under the radar is a full time job, requiring the cooperation of all the preternatural species and quite a few humans as well. On one hand it is easier to hide in plain sight amongst all the naturally accepted weirdness that is New Orleans, but on the other it can get crazy because it is easier to exist in that environment. In the Big Easy no one looks twice at a person with fangs or wings for that matter. There is a parade every weekend and a ghost in every building.

Closing the newspaper with a snap and setting it on the table Kat stood and stretched. It was time to go see Viktor and find out what these new killings meant. She had a hunch that weres were involved, messy killings like this weren't normal by any means. Most likely someone got sloppy and wasn't training their new puppy properly.

Visit my web site or Amazon.com to buy Bad Moon Rising in winter 2013. Thank you for taking the time to enjoy my writing.

Leslie Brown is married and lives in Galveston, Texas. Her husband Kenneth is also a writer and they share their home with 3 dogs and one cat. Their children are grown and they look forward to the golden years together. Leslie is an avid horse rider. Leslie has bachelors in fine art from Sam Houston State University. She taught art for 25 years in the Houston, Texas area, Rio Rancho, New Mexico, and New Orleans, Louisiana. She is currently showing and selling her art in Galveston and previously owned her own gallery in

New Orleans. Visit the web site to find out more information
and see her work.

www.DejaVoodooBook.com
www.LeslieBrownBooks.com

Made in the USA
Middletown, DE
18 February 2022

61272789R00106